The Riddle of Qaf

Aflame Books
2 The Green
Laverstock
Wiltshire
SP1 1QS
United Kingdom
email: info@aflamebooks.com

ISBN: 9781906300036
First published in 2008 by Aflame Books

First published in Portuguese as *O Enigma de Qaf*,
by Editora Record, Rio de Janeiro, 2004.

British Library Cataloguing in Publication Data.
A catalogue record for this book is available from the British Library.

Printed in Poland
www.polskabook.pl

MINISTÉRIO DA CULTURA
Fundação BIBLIOTECA NACIONAL

This work has been published with the support of the
Ministry of Culture of Brazil/National Library Foundation/
Coordenadoria Geral do Livro e da Leitura
Obra publicada com o apoio do Ministério da Cultura do Brasil/
Fundação Biblioteca Nacional /
Coordenadoria Geral do Livro e da Leitura.

The Riddle of Qaf

Alberto Mussa

Translated by Lennie Larkin

Summary

Note of Forewarning

This novel's main story is divided into twenty-eight chapters that are titled according to the twenty-eight letters of the Arabic alphabet.

Between them are intermediary, unnumbered chapters, which I have alternately classified as parameters and excursions.

The excursions are narratives that are more or less related to the main plot, in which they were originally inserted, but which I chose to disassemble for greater appreciation by the reader.

The parameters are legends of Arab heroes who are comparable to the protagonist and poets like him, whose talents you shall be able to judge shortly.

For those merely seeking entertainment in a short tale of adventures (and this is what I advise), you should follow the main story in a linear and direct fashion, and not waste time with the intermediary chapters – which can be saved for later and read at any time and in any order. There is, however, one exception. For a greater understanding of pre-Islamic culture, as well as the mythical universe that envelopes the narrative, it is recommended that you also read the parameters.

Finally, only those who have the gall to try and solve the riddle of Qaf, before reaching the final fullstop, should also read the excursions, and also pay attention to the epigraphs and tidbits of information included beneath each one of the twenty-eight Arabic letters.

١

alif
1st letter
as a number, 1
in a sequence, the 1st
first letter of إلٰه , god, and أللٰه , God

*When I tell a lie,
will I not be restoring
a more ancient truth?*
(Scheherazade, the authentic one)

The Age of Ignorance – as the era that ended with the advent of Islam has come to be known in Arabic history – was a time in which men came to be more noble than horses and mares coveted the beauty of women. It was also a golden age for poets of the desert, who elevated poetry to heights unattained in any language, in any century.

However, as proof of the refined taste of the time, only seven of the poems written during this epoch were transcribed on to camel skins and deemed worthy of being suspended from the great Black Stone which still exists in Mecca, to hang there until made eternal in the memory of the Bedouin.

While in Beirut a few years back, I carried with me a version of an eighth poem that – I maintain – was certainly among those that hung from the great Black Stone. Non-canonical tradition refers to it as *Qafiya al-Qaf*, which can be translated as "poem, whose rhyme is based on the letter *qaf*, which deals with the mountain named Qaf". A play on words, as you can see.

Professors, scholars and intellectuals who have had the privilege of reading the work, confirm that they had never heard of the poem and that they were not at all familiar with either the plot or its characters. I explained that the text was a reconstruction of the original – only as inauthentic as a rock, sculpture, or monument preserved by the hands of a restorer.

The principal objection of these wise men, professors of prestigious universities in Cairo and Beirut, was that there existed no manuscripts which could substantiate my work, nor was I willing to make my sources available.

So it was that I was forced to reveal that I had no sources, if this concept applies only to written material; and that it was my grandfather Naguib who, on falling in love with my grandmother Mari, ran away from home and secretly embarked on the steamship that was carrying Mari's family to Brazil, who carried, besides a suitcase filled only with books, part of the verses of *The Riddle of Qaf*, memorised by heart.

I learnt the essence of the poem from my grandfather. The rest, the gaps that old Naguib's memory did not retain, I recuperated from legends gathered during my wanderings through the Middle East, and from all sorts of diverse historical facts that I was able to compile.

Nevertheless, the text was considered fraudulent. It diverged greatly, I'll admit, in structure and style, from the remaining suspended poems, but it anticipated the technique of composition of imagery that would account for the glory of the language and of the Arab poets. It was certainly this merit that would come to be considered as excessive.

So it was that I never had the honour of publishing the poem; no one would endorse my reconstruction. The versions that circulated (if they had, indeed, circulated, for there exists some doubt about this) were unreliable copies, written in ink on foolscap paper.

As if this weren't enough, a famous scholar of Arabic literature mentioned the case of *Qafiya* as one of the greatest academic forgeries of the Semitic languages.

I was enraged; I went to the newspapers to create an uproar, I called all of those doctors, and I called upon intellectuals of the non-canonical tradition, to defend the poem. Unfortunately, I gradually came to realise that the entire non-canonical tradition was made up of me and me alone.

excursion:

The first Arab

The first time the word *Arab* was written – or, to be more exact, inscribed – to designate a nomad riding atop a camel, was in 853BC, when Jundub and one thousand other men riding camels united Israel and Aram against Assyrian armies.

Historians do not know exactly who this Jundub was, nor the origin of the terrifying Arabs. Jews consider them descendants of Ishmael, the first-born son of Abraham and brother to Isaac. Greeks and Phoenicians agreed that they were sons of Cadmus. The Egyptians, that they had sprung from the sand seasoned by Osiris' sperm. The Persians, that they were Ahriman's faeces.

For Arabs, *Arabs* are all those for whom Arabic is a mother tongue. They are, by this criterion, a single people, albeit divided into hundreds of tribes and lineages of pure and impure Arabs, who cannot necessarily be traced back to a common ancestry.

For the Arabs of the Age of Ignorance, the tribes descended from Ishmael's twelve sons were not Arabs in the written sense of the term. They had been Arabised by the true Arabs, natives of Yemen, from whom they had learnt the language and adopted the customs.

Legends tell of a certain Yarub, who first inhabited the mountains of the south and was the first to herd goats, to burn incense and to prepare the infusion that we know as coffee.

It was also this Yarub who was the first man to speak in Arabic. Except that the Arabic language, unlike all other human languages, did not emerge following the fall of the Tower of Babel. It was invented by Yarub.

At that time, languages comprised just verbs and nouns, as well as a few minor pronouns and articles. Yarub created the adjective. But he was not satisfied.

"I want an infinite language, in which each word has infinite synonyms," goes the classic phrase.

And Yarub's indefatigable work made Arabic an infinite language. But there was a problem: he substituted one word for another without ever obtaining the same meaning, in a precise, exact, unequivocal manner. There always arose a new idea, a variation, something that diverged from the original sense.

It was the case of *jamal* (camel), initially a synonymous pretense of *jameel* (beauty); or of *bayt* (house), which Yarub tried to implement as the equivalent of *bayd* (egg).

Unfortunately, these failures trickled into popular understanding and inspired the first vagabonds who began to write poetry. Yarub armed men to silence them. But he was unsuccessful: the vice of poetry had contaminated the women; and they came to hide the fugitive men, throwing their own clothes over them as they took them off.

Yarub confronted this shame and continued the siege until one of the poets – Awad, pronounced also as Awad – composed the satire in which the same term could have two meanings. It was the end.

"The words are not even synonyms of themselves," he concluded, with eyes low.

At this point, the versions contradict one another, but what is certain is that Yarub withdrew from human company, and in the solitude of the mountains he sought to achieve perfection in his language.

He was alone for twenty-eight years. His beard and hair grew so long that he would have been unrecognisable, were he not the one person still capable of inventing vocabulary, from one moment to the next, to discover something with semantically identical results to its predecessor and possess a single signified.

Already on the edge of death, after having infinitely failed, he called his children together so as to redeem himself.

"I don't believe in synonyms."

And he spoke not one more word.

ب

ba
2nd letter
as a number, 2
in a sequence, the 2ⁿᵈ
first letter of بكارة, hymen, and باب, door

> *Two types write:*
> *those with no memory;*
> *those with no words.*
> (Anonymous)

The journey that brought the poet, author of *Qafiya* and this novel's hero, to solve the riddle of Qaf, was the same as that which gave him the love of Layla. I cannot, therefore, deny a place in eternity to the camel skin that first recorded this story, although I know that there are few who truly value its knowledge and beauty.

Of her, of Layla, there might not be much that has remained. But at least I shall bestow immortality on the name of the poet al-Ghatash and on the tribe of Labwa, I shall reconstitute the most beautiful of the poems, I shall reveal the interpretation of the most fascinating of the riddles, I shall dispel legends of the skills of genies and the power of gods. Because it has to be thus; those free of vanity do not write books.

I learnt the legend of al-Ghatash while still young, while sitting at the foot of my grandfather's rocking chair, alone with him, in the old clothing factory in the depths of the huge house on Rua Formosa, in Campos dos Goytacazes. Old Naguib recited to me, in Portuguese, that which I assume was his personal adaptation of *Qafiya*.

From the first time I heard it, I was fascinated by this story of a poet who crossed the desert in search of an unknown woman, of a riddle that told of a fabled circular mountain, of a blind and cross-eyed genie who could travel through time.

I remember well my grandfather's emotion in that rocking chair. I sensed that he believed in the legend of the riddle, in the possibility of men like us, men of flesh and blood, returning to the past. Whenever I began to doubt, he would look at me, deadly serious, and would point to a dusty instrument, which I later came to discover was a small telescope.

My grandfather Naguib died before teaching me what a telescope was. I grew up with the poem ingrained in my memory – that is obvious. But I wanted it in a written version. I turned the house on Rua Formosa upside down, searched through trunks, opened each one of the five thousand volumes on the bookshelves, I even knocked over the telescope, and all I found were a few loose pages, which bore the handwriting of Naguib and recorded only brief observations on Arabic literature, with no mention of the adventure of al-Ghatash or the blind, cross-eyed genie.

There was also a sketch of our family tree – tracing us back to descendants of the tribe of Labwa, settled since the fifth century in the deserts that surround the hills of Hebron.

It was this desire to salvage the lost fragments and to give written form to *Qafiya* that inspired me to learn classical Arabic, Hebrew, the myriad Syrian dialects, and even the extinct epigraphical idiom of Yemen. I also immersed myself in the archaeology of the Middle East; I pored over the geography of the deserts of Syria and Arabia; I studied Bedouin ethnology; and practically learnt pre-Islamic poetry by heart.

But it was only when I dedicated myself to the science of the stars, in the primitive fashion that arose among the Chaldeans, that I could reconstruct the original poem and come to solve the riddle of Qaf.

parameter:

Imru al-Qays

For a large majority of scholars, the most ancient recognised Arab poet is Imru al-Qays, and not al-Ghatash.

There are some important distinctions between them: Al-Qays was the son of the powerful chief of the Kinda tribe; as for al-Ghatash, we do not know who his father was. Al-Qays is not linked with any female figure; while al-Ghatash was obsessed with Layla. It was al-Qays' spirit that received and guided the prophet Muhammad on his visit to the circles of hell; al-Ghatash would not have had any such patience.[1]

Al-Qays was reckless. There are those who say he had the eyes of a year-old calf and that, with these eyes, he seduced countless women. While in Constantinople, he even made love to the virgin daughter of Caesar himself, between the very palace walls and under the noses of the Byzantine guards. He crept into encampments at night to kidnap lovers. He was particularly fond of surprising naked girls while they bathed in the oasis. Al-Qays possessed true passion.

At the beginning of his Suspended Poem, he enumerates various abandoned encampments, where he would stop and cry at

---

1. It has been said that the Florentine plagiarist Dante Alighieri profusely studied Muslim eschatology before writing his Comedy, and that he gave Imru al-Qays the Latin name of Virgil.

the memory of a woman and of tents, searching for footprints erased by the desert winds.

He never gives the name of the beloved who inspired him, as convention of the genre determines. Critics assume he is referring to a Bedouin woman who moved on to inhabit the locations mentioned. But no: at each stop in the desert there was another love for al-Qays.

It was his own father who banished him from the tribe, on learning that his son had been caressing what throbbed beneath his own cousin's tunic, after jumping on his camel and bursting into the palanquin.

And I said: go ahead, free the rein, but do not take from me this fruit that shall harvest double...

This adventure was, in one sense, the last straw. It seems that the poet's father was already enraged by some verses that were circulating and revealed the sexual exploits of al-Qays. The scene in which he has his way with a pregnant girl at the same time as she breastfeeds a baby has a disgusting beauty.

In the erotic prelude common to all classic poems, it is rare for a poet to exceed a dozen or so verses. Al-Qays composed more than forty.

But this sexual hypertrophy did not lead to a disregard of other traditional motifs: the glorification of the horse, the sacrifice of the camel, the hunting scenes, the description of the desert. Certain images are impressive, like that of nightfall, compared to the chest of a black charger that jumps and tumbles over the horseman.

The originality of al-Qays' poem lies, moreover, in the description of the enveloping storm which is, according to some, a foreshadow of the Apocalypse. In the midst of the fury of the elements, where the mountains are the heads of weaving spindles, the drowned wild animals are onion roots, the fallen trees are paprika powder, Imru al-Qays' most beautiful verse resounds:

In Tayma not a palm tree was left standing; and among the structures of stone, only cliffs.

In these passages, one perceives that al-Qays was a man of great solitude. In vain they have tried to discover if there was not a woman, at least one, whom he had loved more profoundly.

They searched for traces in the Suspended Poem itself, trying to recompose the picture of the Bedouin woman whose hair adorns her back, thick and black, like a cluster of dates on a heavily laden palm tree; whose waistline is a fine cord; whose legs are reeds of papyrus on the marsh; whose fingers, when they move, are white larvae, or fine twigs.

And I ask: would women of the desert be beautiful if they were not just like this?

I believe that the most beautiful verse of poetry in all the universe could be this, attributed to al-Qays:

When the constellation of Pleiades appeared in the sky like a necklace of shining pearls,
I entered, suddenly, the tent; and she, before the curtain, undressing, for bed, except for the most intimate garment...
and I pressed myself against her – and a skirt slid to sweep away the tracks we left behind...

I am still the only person on this earth to doubt the authenticity of these verses. They have already asserted that this is spite on my part, that I attempt to make of al-Qays that which others have made of al-Ghatash. They are liars. I am quite familiar with the personality of al-Qays. It does not seem right to me that he would allow the footsteps of that woman to be swept away, notwithstanding the risk of being discovered by the girl's uncles. They say that he was passionate about form. He loved the imprint of a body in the sand more than he loved the woman who had been lying there.

ج

jeem
5th letter
as a number, 3
in a sequence, the 3rd
first letter of جمال, beauty, and جنة, insanity

I love women who,
undressed, are never,
completely, naked.
(Imru al-Qays)

The eyes of the sons of Ghurab did not look upon me with benevolence, as I dismounted from my camel, brushed off the dust that covered my white tunic, and demanded the hospitality of those of the desert. The women appeared from behind curtains of braided hair, which set the harem apart, and pulled their veils over their faces, like gazelles fleeing from lions.[2] The men did not move from their mats.

"Arise, Arabs! I am al-Ghatash, of the tribe of Labwa. For eleven days I have been travelling alone in the footsteps of this animal."

Rocks could not have rivalled their silence. Only the wind dared rustle the tunics and billow the tents. A few mares, of the purest

---

2. Labwa, in Arabic, is one of the infinite synonyms of 'lioness'.

breeds of Arabia, of those which accounted for the Ghurab's wealth, whinnied in my direction.

"I will pay any price for such an animal!"

And I advanced towards the encampment, as if those men were but tufts of grass on a dry river's edge. When the first of the mares made to approach me, al-Muthanni, the sheik, fell on me, sword in hand: "No stranger violates the chastity of the daughters of Ghurab!"

Because there emerged, from among the mares that suckled foals, a woman of the tribe; and the wind, in a stronger gust, loosened her veil.

The mares of Ghurab sang: the black manes, the thick lips, the wide hips. Not one of them could compare to the girl who had just seduced me.

"Sheik of the Ghurab, I will have the most perfect mare, who was formed under your very own tent!"

Al-Muthanni smiled, because I acknowledged recognising the sheik's own daughter. However, behind us, a sword in each fist, someone snarled:

"From whose tribe is this thief who dares come and request Dhu Suyef's betrothed?"

I turned to meet his gaze, with disdain:

"He is al-Ghatash; and this here is my scimitar. Those who have dared rouse the wrath of my tribe are now rotting beneath the earth."

His response was lost, drowned out by the whinnying of the mares.

excursion:

The dyke of Marib

Innumerable are the books affirming that Arabs are originally from the desert. This is not true. Before they inhabited the dry sands, on occasion drinking salty well water, having at times to consume just milk in order to save the water for the camels, these men inhabited cities. With time, they went in search of more temperate regions, confined to the south of the peninsula, and they learnt to divert the course of rivers and build dams.

It is strange that in historic times, tribes that descended from these opulent citizens then became nomads and came to wander the lands of Syria and Iraq. One legend tells the story of this migration.

In Marib, in Yemen, was the most fabulous of these dykes, that supplied not just the city of Marib but also many coastal villages from the Red Sea to the edges of the Arabian Sea.

Rich and powerful, the people of Marib negotiated with foreign rulers and would receive in the tents merchants from India, Persia, Egypt, Phoenicia, Abyssinia, Babylon.

But it was a unique commerce, in which the merchandise was bought and sold only by means of gestures. It is not that the foreigners did not speak Arabic: they were not able to make sense of the phrases pronounced in Marib.

For the people of Marib spoke only in symbols. It was considered undignified to employ a language that had not been configured in symbols.

Therefore, if anyone wished to speak of a camel, they could refer to it as "ship" or "dune". They could use "rat" to mean "dagger"; and "eye" instead of "oasis". Sometimes, whole phrases such as "I need to kiss your sandals", in place of "I want a goblet of wine".

The paths of these metaphors were sometimes simple, as in the association between "eye" and "oasis", because water flows from both; or between "camel" and "ship", because the ocean is a type of desert; even that between "rat" and "dagger", because the teeth of the one have a sharp point like the blade of the other.

However, normally, these successions of similes were somewhat more complicated, thus making it necessary to know, for example, that the wine of Marib was imported on the backs of camels, and that it was these animals that supplied the leather used to make footwear; or to have seen sand dunes moved by desert winds, similar to camel's hunchbacks as they recede gradually through the desert.

But there was a day on which one of the farmers of Marib appeared in the city centre and screamed:

"There is a crack on the wall of the dyke!"

Immediately, a woman stabbed her husband, imagining that "dyke" symbolised a man swollen with desire, that "wall" was his rigidity, and "crack" the obvious metaphor of which we are all aware. Besides her, no one seemed to pay much attention.

In truth, the sentence did not make much sense. No one was able to interpret it satisfactorily. The farmer repeated it in a loud voice, some three or four times, before fleeing Marib, heading in the direction of Syria.

The next day, the dyke collapsed. The flood killed a great many people. The city and surrounding villages were destroyed. A great majority of the survivors initiated an exodus towards the north.

They tried in vain to find the man who had spoken this sentence, whose literal terms had cunningly eluded the people of Marib. But they would have committed an injustice, had they caught him.

Anxious, desperate, with the pure intention of warning the people of Marib, in searching for an unequivocal symbol for the concepts of "crack" and "dyke", the man ran through the entire

Arabic vocabulary, word by word, until closing the circle, choosing "crack" as a metaphor for "crack"; and "dyke" as a metaphor for "dyke".

 د

dhal
8th letter
as a number, 4
in a sequence, the 4th
first letter of دير, temple, and دم, blood

Honour does not pass
as an aspect of fear.
(Shanfara)

Flashes made by the hooves of the Ghurab's black mares as they struck desert rocks, on a starless night, did not shine as brightly as the sparks made by the scimitars of al-Ghatash and Dhu Suyuf, the man of two sabres – an allusion to his impressive ability to fight with a weapon in each hand.[3]

The bleary eyes of the men of Ghurab, obscured in their dark tunics, were all on the sheik, like falcons spying rats. For al-Muthanni's tolerance was strange: even allowing for the tribal right to hospitality, al-Ghatash could not have risked approaching the harem with impunity.

But such was the fascinating part of this eloquence, that

---

3. My detractors have pointed out an error here: the correct expression for "the man of two sabres" is Dhu Sayfayn, using the Arabic dual plural, and not Dhu Suyuf, which is the plural for more than two. I have desisted from arguing that poetic licence is common, principally for adequacy in poetic metre.

al-Ghatash took it a step further: challenging the terrifying Dhu Suyuf for his betrothed.

The combat, too, was strange: Dhu Suyuf, so honorable that he wished not to wound a guest within the limits of the encampment, merely deflected the poet's blows. At a certain point, al-Ghatash would have protested:

"This is an unequal fight. He has two swords. I, only one!"

Dhu Suyuf, then, fought with one sword in his left hand, merely brushing aside al-Ghatash's attacks. After some time had passed, the poet insisted:

"This is an unequal fight. I am fighting with my right hand. He, with his left!"

Dhu Suyuf switched to defending himself from al-Ghatash's attempts with a sabre in his right hand.

Many were the times at which al-Ghatash could have fallen; Dhu Suyuf did not once try to strike him. Perhaps he was seeking a dual victory: to maintain ownership of his betrothed while not violating the right to hospitality.

The wind, however, did not let up. Al-Ghatash must have noticed that the gusts had intensified and were churning up more sand. So, he turned his back to the wind and fell to his knees, elbows on the ground, forehead to the earth.

Dhu Suyuf, thinking that al-Ghatash had fallen from exhaustion, believing he had won, extended his hand to the guest. And herein lies the mystery: because Dhu Suyuf got up quickly to escape his opponent's sudden attack, incapable of defending himself for he had put down his sword and held both hands over his eyes, which were full of sand blown by the wind or else thrown by the hands of the poet al-Ghatash.

parameter:

Antara

The mythical figures of al-Ghatash and Antara are easily confused. Antara was the greatest of heroes: al-Ghatash, the greatest of poets. And, among Arabs, every hero is a poet; every poet is a hero.

But there are, certainly, differences. Al-Ghatash was passionate about mares; Antara loved just one horse.

Antara's mother was an Ethiopian slave, and his father kept him in a state of servitude. When a conflict erupted between two of the tribe's great clans – precisely because of a dispute over a horse race – Antara was ordered by his own father to take up arms and fight.

He refused, it seems, saying that the role of servants was to take care of the camels. Antara's father, to his son's surprise, freed him; and the son of the Ethiopian, in this and subsequent battles, was compelled to fight, like a lion.

Historians have identified a deception in this gesture, in forcing his inclusion in the paternal lineage. I disagree: Antara knew that no one would go to war without him; what he wanted was to spare the horses. This passion for animals shines through in the bloodier scenes:

When I saw the enemies approaching, inciting each other, I turned on them, but I was not wounded.

"Antara!" they screamed, and in my black stallion's chest the
spears were like taut ropes, hoisting a bucket from a deep well;
If he had known how to speak, he would have complained; had
he made use of words, I would have come to understand.

They say that Antara loved one, and only one, horse. The
legend adds yet one further passion: Abla, his cousin, who came
from a rival clan – according to some – or, according to others,
was denied Antara by his uncle, who did not want grandchildren
with dark skin.

In my opinion, Abla never loved Antara. I doubt that she was
ever loved by him. There was, between the two, an animal
attraction as in those seeking out the most perfect of their species.
In all the passages that speak of this supposed love for his cousin,
there is always the shadow of a horse.

Did poets leave behind anything that was not perfect? Or did
you recognise, in the images, the abandoned encampment?
I dismounted from my horse, as from the tower of a fortress, to
kill the anguish of those who remained.

In much literature, the image of the tower of an unconquerable
castle is the conventional metaphor for impossible love. When he
speaks undoubtedly of his cousin, he insinuates doubtful
sentiments:

I fell in love by chance, while my relatives killed it...

In another famous passage, Antara compares Abla's smile to
the glistening blade of a sword; and the freshness of her kiss, to
a fertile plain, unsullied by animals, under vernal clouds whose
fine rain leaves small pools, almost like silver coins.

The reviewers committed an error here. The final part is an
image by al-Ghatash. Antara made silver coins with the drops of
sweat from his horse.

But love of horses is love of war. Antara was a magnificent
narrator of battles. He killed his enemies with a slash to the
jugular, done in such a way as to resemble a leper's lip, and he left

the body to serve as a guide to the jackals. I remember that Antara also had a leper's lip: it was as if he had stamped his seal on the body.

It is said that he compared Abla's smile to the blade of a sword. It is curious that the ferocity of his enemy could provoke in him the same simile:

It is these men who, while watching me dismount, bare their teeth, with something that is not a smile...

It is highly unlikely, if not impossible, that a proud man such as Antara loved a woman who disdained him or was descended from enemy blood. In place of an unattainable love, he lived in search of the inexorable end in the field of combat.

Antara died from an arrow to the base of his spine. He was mounted on his horse, Abjar, ready to descend into the valley and attack the rival clan. The concealed archer ran back to give news of the hero's death. But Abjar, with Antara's body on its back, also ran, in the same direction.

And they saw Antara and Abjar. And they fled, but not before first executing the archer, for having relayed what they believed to be a false message.[4]

Antara's body wandered for some time, captive on Abjar's saddle, putting the enemies to flight, until it decomposed and, eventually, fell to the ground. No one knows if it was buried. But Abjar continues galloping, to this very day, over the desert sands.

I once saw this horse. None of Antara's verses is as beautiful as that horse.

---

4. This scene was related in Spain and impressed the rhapsodists who narrated the story of El-Cid Campeador.

ه

huh
26th letter
as a number, 5
in a sequence, the 5th
first letter of هوى, passion, and هجرة, exile

*Not all numbers
are multiples of one.*
(Yarub)

The adventure which led al-Ghatash to discover and solve the riddle of Qaf began at the moment when the sheik of the Ghurab, during an assembly of the tribe's men, rose suddenly and left, pushing aside those in his path, until he halted in front of a tall tent that was covered in red cloths with tassels of black fleece.

"Answer, Sabah! Which of the two is less deserving of you!"

Al-Ghatash had offered a bride price of two hundred and twenty camels, to be handed over in Mecca, during the month of pilgrimage. One of Dhu Suyuf's old uncles, gesticulating wildly and slapping his own face, was still courageous enough to invoke the previously established agreement. The sheik lifted his right hand to his cummerband:

"Sabah has made her choice. The foreigner won a fair duel. And there are no more poets in the tribe of Ghurab."

Severe, the looks the Ghurab shot at al-Muthanni.

Indescribable, those of Dhu Suyuf – his face covered in bandages, having been wounded by al-Ghatash while he withdrew, blinded by the sand, regretting not having killed the guest.

And then the tent opened; and a strong odour of musk reached the men. It was Sabah, who came from the bride's gathering dressed in silk vestments and covered in jewels, after a long nuptial bath. The desert wind blew strongly against her. Her veil, once again, came unfastened, and her tunic formed shapes as rounded and beautiful as the letters of the scribes.

Old Naguib particularly loved al-Ghatash's verses on this occasion:

"Her body stemmed from two trunks of Lebanese cedar, reaching a summit covered in thick grass. And he who lay down in front of this lawn would see the circle of a camel's light footprint, alone in the undulating and white plain, with two great trembling dunes in the distance ."

I believe these lines led them to imagine that al-Ghatash spoke of Sabah. I suppose that the Ghurab made the same error.

However, al-Ghatash sang of the veiled figure of Layla, who came behind, combing the hair of her sister Sabah, while also, perchance being sculpted by the wind.

excursion:

The disappearance of Samira

From the south of the Arabian Peninsula two important routes head towards the Fertile Crescent, travelled upon since Antiquity by the caravans that transported incense, myrrh, precious stones, the riches of Ethiopia and the marvels of India.

One of these follows the coast of the Red Sea, connecting Yemen to Syria and Palestine, passing through Mecca. The other follows the shores of the Persian Gulf, from Oman to the south of Iraq, continuing along the Euphrates as far as the old Assyrian territory.

Since the most remote of times, almost all the primitive Arabs, who came from Yemen, emigrated by one of these routes, imposing the Arabic language on the tribes of the north, with whom they interbred.

On this passage, many were lost, giving birth to legends of forgotten tribes and cities sunk in the sands.

It is said that one of the most inhospitable Arabian deserts sheltered a tribe lost in its impenetrable immensity. They were said to be of the lineage of Bilqis, queen of Sheba, and it was said that the men were ferocious; and the women well-formed.

Of Samira, the matriarch, it spread that she possessed the most beautiful face of all humanity, although no one had ever seen it.

Arabs from all corners of the world pursued the women of this tribe. Those fortunate enough to glimpse them insisted on the fact that they did not possess a common beauty. They were the most gorgeous women; of a perfection never seen in the peninsula, nor in the entire surrounding universe.

Sometimes, they were met in casual encounters, when they emerged intermittently from the desert to get closer to less arid lands and to liberate a goat or steal a camel. And other times, by hidden Bedouins who tried to capture them. They all died, generally, at the bloody hands of tribal men.

On one occasion, however, a group of six or seven men attacked a few tents belonging to the tribe of Samira, relegated to the confines of the fertile lands of Hadramut. Captured and tied one to the other like stones in a necklace, they were taken to stand before Samira herself, the most beautiful of women, whom they did not expect to encounter on such a fringe of the desert.

Facing her, the men's discomfort was visible. Victims of some type of curse, they lost their sense of direction, incapable of walking in a straight line or of finding their own way.

In this shameful state, they were dragged some distance hence, where they were abandoned.

It is not known whether it was by chance, or if the distance covered by the tribe was small: the fact is that one of these men showed up again on the edge of Samira's uninhabitable desert, just before dying of thirst.

The story he must have told encouraged new persecutions, and Samira's tribe became beseiged, confined to the dry, ruddy, impassable land.

One day, in a marketplace in Qatar, three men appeared, pulling a camel by its reins. On the animal's hump, a woman, completely covered by veils, with just her hands peeking through the Persian tunic that covered her from head to toe.

"It's Samira," said one of them.

The men of Qatar gathered that Samira's captors were half dazed, that they did not take note of anything, and they tripped over their own feet, banging their foreheads together.

It was then that the reins broke or she somehow freed herself. Samira, veiled, flogged the camel on and vanished into the desert, for good.

As was later remarked, they were blind, all three of them. It is not known if this was from before or after having seen Samira. It is not known for how long she had been using that veil.

و

waw
27th letter
as a number, 6
in a sequence, the 6th
first letter of وحخ, refuge, and ودع, grave

Is there no glory greater
than to be mocked by hyenas?
(Amru bin Kulthum)

"Son of the sons of Labwa, put Sabah on your camel and leave! Enemies do not last long among the men of Ghurab!"

That is how they bade me farewell. And they seated Sabah at my back. A hundred and ten curses on men who do not respect the three days of hospitality. A hundred and ten times eleven curses on the rival who preferred to endure dishonour rather than face the point of my sabre.

For twenty-two days I searched for the Labwa's whereabouts. I never stopped turning my head to admire the face of that woman whom each breeze threatened to unveil. I penetrated her in the desert, between the howling of jackals and the shrieking of hyenas. But I did not see anything in that likeness without mystery.

For I thought of Layla, whom I had not seen without her veils:

calf with black eyes like two pools of bitumen that sprout from the belly of the earth.

"I will have two hundred and twenty camels delivered to Mecca during the month of pilgrimage, to the tribe of Ghurab, as a bride price for this woman, whom I have rejected. And four hundred and forty more are added as bride price for the woman whom I seek."

This is what I said to the assembly of the sons of Labwa, throwing Sabah into their midst. And I travelled through the desert, with no regard for my camel that was burning up in the sun.

Salty was the water that I stole from wells. I did not pass any caravans that I could pillage. I was surrounded, instead, by sand dunes. But the crescent moon put vagabonds in my path, and they would have robbed me if I had not offered them something to drink.

"Get off your camel, Arab! Men without a tribe can also be generous."

We stopped under the sky, wrapped in old and stinking blankets. The curd they gave me was rotten. The bread already had a bit of mould. I realised that my abused camel had not had much to drink; and I spotted next to him a younger animal, with chubby and beautiful thighs, loaded with two camel skin bags of dirty water, in addition to having udders full of milk.

It was this very animal that I led away, by the reins, in silence, taking the rest of the food, while they slept.

But a rock made the beast stumble. The sound of water that sloshed about in the water bag woke up the band and, before I could reach for my bow, I had been caught. Their sheik pulled me by the hair.

"How curious: the ingrates I have met have been very similar from the neck up. Umar, my sword!"

However, just then a wave of dust darkened the night. The harsh wind demolished the encampment and extinguished the fire. With eyes full of sand, I could not see, but just the same I threw myself on to the camel and used my turban to cover my eyes.

I cannot say whether or not they followed me. But, amid the

boom of thunder, I sensed a hollow, resonating voice, emerging perhaps from the depths of time, echoing behind me:

"The poet of Labwa is in the right. This camel is the granddaughter of another, stolen by Umar, that had once belonged to Jalila, mother of al-Ghatash."

parameter:

Nabigha

In nature, no two creatures are alike. It has long been known that this also applies to twins. Recently, however, certain stories of people who have come face-to-face with their perfect copies, or with their 'doubles', revived the myth. But they are no more than abominable lies, and should be banned.

On the contrary, the truth is that each being has an antithesis, an antipode, an anti-twin. Such was the case with two Arab princes: Amru and Numan.

One was an ally to the Greeks; the other, to the Persians. One was thin; the other fat. One of them had light eyes; the eyes of the other were as black as night. They were both ugly, but for one it was due to a nose defect; the other, due to his ears. And both were praised by Nabigha the poet. It was this occurrence that made them famous.

Nabigha was not descended from poets. A convert to Christianity, he went to live in the court of Numan, allied to the Persians, and there learnt to compose panegyrics that granted him a place among the luminaries of classic poetry. From Numan, he obtained everything, ever since reciting the first verse of his Suspended Poem:

Mayya's dwelling, in the mountains of Samad and Aliya, deserted, where the past elapses forever...

The description of the camel, whose teeth were as sharp and precise as fish hooks, also left an impression on the prince; he was reminded of a wild bull from the plains, with a stomach curved like a scimitar, that launches ferociously into the hunting dogs and turns and twists with one on its horns, like a piece of meat on a roasting skewer.

Nabigha compared Numan to his camel; and subsequently, to that bull. Not one sovereign of Numan's lineage had ever received a more vehement eulogy. And the prince requested Nabigha to compose a poem about each member of his extended family.

The poem about Mutajarrida, Numan's wife, narrated the moment at which she emerged from the tent, like a gazelle with a radiant face, her torso perfect like that of a palm that balances above the trees in the forest. Nabigha compared her to the rising sun, to a pearl of the ocean, to a marble statue on a stone pedestal.

It was bold, when he added a scene in which the girl's veil fell and she, timid, hid her face with one of her hands, while trying to grasp the piece of silk: delicate fingers tinted rouge like lotus buds, her black and undulating braids expanding like an arbour's vines, her eyes imploring like someone incarcerated...

Numan, proud, did not seem upset. Until rumours began to spread that the images of Nabigha were too perfect. Immediately, it was taken as fact that the poet could only have described that which he must have seen; or experienced. This plausible theory was Nabigha's ruin. Because Numan remembered the metaphor of the bull, and, because he considered himself a bull, he also thought that Nabigha had contemplated Mutajarrida's naked beauty.

Nabigha was exiled and arrived at the court of Prince Amru, allied to the Greeks. The story was not much different: Nabigha did not delay in ingratiating himself with the prince. Famous, rightly so, is the poem that was composed in his honour.

In it, Amru's troops are preceded by battalions of vultures, which opened the way for the men – old companions who were akin to hunting dogs, raised to look upon blood without fear. It is these vultures that congregate around the arena, like old men wearing black, aware of the enemies who fall in front of the tribe in which not one defect exists, except that of the sabres, which have tempered blades.

But Nabigha's old poems also ended up being circulated, including the one about Mutajarrida. It did not take long for rumours to spread about Nabigha and Amru's wife, whom they assumed to be the woman described in the poem.

Prince Amru, nevertheless, had complete faith in the woman, and exiled the poet. He, too, had heard that Nabigha could only describe that which he had seen. He concluded that the poems were mere lies. That Nabigha had just composed verses of pure fantasy; that – if Amru's woman was faithful – he, Amru, did not deserve all that glory; that he, Amru, had more defects than just chinks on the blade of his sword.

ز

zay
11th letter
as a number, 7
in a sequence, the 7th
first letter of زان, adulterer, and زكي, honoured one

> *Three are the fools:*
> *he who knows not that he knows not;*
> *he who knows that he knows not;*
> *he who knows not that he knows.*
> (Labid)

"Mr Mussa, there does not exist in Arab mythology, there is no reference in any of the ancient texts, nor in al-Biruni's treatise, nor in ibn Nadim's index, nor in the work of Chafic Maluf – who was the greatest modern authority on this subject – a genie named Jadah. Nor did there exist a blind or cross-eyed genie, who lives in the past and returns to the present in sand storms, pronouncing testimonies that he cannot prove. There is not even an etymology for this name, not a single plausible root in any of the Semitic languages. I fear that your fantasies have crossed the line."

Professor Yahia was one of those who argued the *Qafiya*'s inauthenticity, one of the 'inauthenticists', as they came to be known. He even went so far as to present the problem in a conference of Arabists. Unfortunately, I relied on him to obtain my degree in pre-Islamic literature.

"Professor Yahia, have you consulted *The Book of the Cave Monastery?*"

I received the negative answer I had expected. I then explained to him, trying to appear modest, that this work – a Syrian chronicle of a famous monastery in the vicinity of the Arabic city of Petra – of which only fragments remain, was the only one to mention the mythical figure of Jadah.

According to the anonymous author, Jadah was a gigantic genie, who had a rumbling voice and was blind in one eye. When Alexander the Great began his conquest of the Orient, he was one of the supernatural beings who intervened against the advance of the terrifying Macedonian.

He lost the battle, in hand-to-hand combat against Alexander himself, who stabbed him right in the face and withdrew, bearing one eye skewered on his sword.

Jadah, nevertheless, would not be defeated. In a spectacular move, he assumed the form and texture of smoke and emptied himself beyond the peaks of Qaf mountain, in order to go back in time and recover the eye. Bedouins are particularly afraid of sand storms that blow from the confines of the earth, for Jadah may be hidden in them; and the testimony of he who comes from yesterday can never be put to the test.

"If what you say, sir, is true, I would like to know in which library I can find this work."

"I'm very sorry. It is a shame, sir, that you have not had time to go through all of the existing ancient manuscripts in your own university."

We descended to the rare documents section. The librarian brought us a grubby index card with the Syrian title *The Book of the Cave Monastery*. The cataloguing followed all bibliographic norms. In the annotations, there was only my own signature, proving that I had been the only one to request it.

But I could not suppress my outrage when we discovered that that manuscript, that paleographic rarity, could no longer be found on the shelf indicated on the index card. The staff went through everything, to no avail.

"The Lebanese schools are famous for being taken seriously, Professor Yahia."

The man was beside himself.

"I'm going to order an investigation into this index card, Mr Mussa! This reeks of fraud! And I'll tell you something else: you look ridiculous in that Italian suit and a Bedouin turban!"

I was on the verge of muttering something about cultural roots, but he had just slammed the door shut.

The next day, I caught the plane to São Paulo. I never learnt of the result of the investigation.

excursion:

The two mirrors

Arabs were among the first people to adopt Christianity, even though many tribes remained pagans or maintained certain traditional religious rites. There were many Arabs among the first Christian martyrs. The first Roman emperor to accept being baptised was Phillip, quite rightly called 'the Arab'. Arab bishops were present in the councils that debated famed Byzantine matters, aligned with the Orthodox block. The two most ancient inscriptions in the Arabic language, preserved today, were inscribed in Christian churches.

In truth, it was the tribes of the desert who conceived of Christianity, two centuries before Christ himself.

It is not known exactly when it spread, but it was certainly a relatively ancient practice, that between Semites, it was customary to sacrifice the first-born son, to placate the divine fury against the tribe or to ingratiate the father to a divinity. No one is ignorant, for example, of the story of Isaac and Abraham.

Between Bedouins, it was not any different.

When misery and disease chose a certain Adib, a maker of mirrors, an oracle demanded the blood of his first son.

Adib laughed, then cried, for he had only daughters. Desperate, believing the idol expected the impossible precisely to avoid having to help him, he withdrew into the desert, and went to await death.

The idea came to him when, in a gesture of self commiseration, he put his own face to the mirror of his sceptre. Although he had worked with mirrors for years, he had never noticed the fact that the image reflected was an inversion of the actual appearance: the right side of his face appeared in the left side of the mirror, and vice versa. To obtain a perfect reflection, a second mirror was necessary – or as it is, two inversions of the original figure.

Such was Adib's thinking: if Allah demands my oldest son, I can satisfy him by offering my youngest daughter.

And this is just what he did. And Adib lived and prospered. The news spread rapidly, and several tribes began, collectively, to prefer to sacrifice their last-born. The Koran condemned this custom, which demonstrated that it was in vogue in the seventh century.

But the speculation with respect to the double reflection did not end there. There were some who continued to make inversions, not always well-grounded, offering the oldest wife in place of the youngest daughter; or an in-law; or a niece.

In time, discussions on the subject came to be merely theoretical, and desert scholars proposed an innovative double inversion: if, originally, the father's life was equivalent to the son's death (the presupposition of the double reflex being present), the life of man, in general, would also be equal to the death of a god.

The great impetus that the cult of Adonis (a god who dies) achieved in the Hellenistic period, perhaps, has something to do with this thesis. But this is not important.

The fact is that the principles of the doctrine were established: if the god Allah can be defined as the Divine Father, the death of the Divine Father must be equivalent to the death of the Human Son. And if this Son has blood spilt, no one could cause his mother's blood to run; or rather, the mother will be a virgin.

For two hundred years, Bedouins wandered about the oases, villages and cities, searching for a human son of Allah's, born to a virgin. It was not by chance that three Arab princes (known later and erroneously as "the Magi") identified the birth of a boy with these characteristics.

There are, however, those who affirm that this is a case of

mistaken identity. That there is no solid proof regarding the baby's paternity. That the mirrors can be turned in another direction.

ح
ha
6th letter
as a number, 8
in a sequence, the 8th
first letter of حب, love, and حجاب, veil

To respect enemies
is to idolise the dead.
(Antara)

It is the *Book of the Cave Monastery* that documents the tribe of al-Muthanni's last march, from the Syrian steppes to the confines of Arabia, where he had to recover from his disgrace. At the time of these events, perhaps in the middle of the fifth century, the tribes of the north were more or less converted to Christianity, as opposed to the Ghurab and some others, who were still firmly rooted in the traditional religion.

The Ghurab kept up a blood feud against Salih's powerful tribe, unswerving Orthodoxes, who could count on Constantinople's support.

The *Book* tells the story of Dhu Suyuf, who, while invading enemy territory to steal water, ambushed and killed, at the same time as two sons of Bulbul, the sheik of Salih. The Ghurab encampment was then attacked by horsemen under the command of the sheik himself.

Taken by surprise, the Ghurab would lose the battle; but Bulbul, in a frenzy of hatred, wielding a terrible Persian scimitar, had his horse stand over the body of al-Muthanni (who had been fighting on foot), reared his horse; and, when he went to complete the blow, the Ghurab sheik picked a fallen spear off the ground and sunk it into the horse's stomach, impaling Bulbul.

The Salih despaired and beat a retreat. The Ghurab took the defeated sheik's body and delivered it to two of al-Muthanni's servants, embalmers captured in the Egyptian desert.

For this was the Ghurab's custom: to save, protected under the sheik's own tent, the mummified bodies of his enemies.

But al-Muthanni could not resist the fury of Salih, who invoked the alliance of Kalb, Tnukh, Bahrá, Tayy, Ghassan and Jusham. The Ghurab began their flight to the south, carrying with them, embalmed, the body of Bulbul.

The Salih horsemen set off into the desert, in the Ghurab's tracks. They discovered traces of an abandoned encampment. It is here where they will encounter al-Ghatash, after having been saved by Jadah's testimony.

The poet, crouching at the side of a camel, brushes away, delicately, with his hands, the finest layers of sand, trying to identify signs of Layla beneath. The men of Salih would have then acted mercilessly, had the Labwa not also been a converted tribe. And al-Ghatash accompanied them.

They entered the dangerous Desert of Mirages. This was not an ordinary desert. They were not ordinary mirages. Instead of perceiving water where there was sand, in the Desert of Mirages the Bedouins saw sand where there was water – and they followed it without pause, only to die of thirst many leagues later.

There was a moment at which they did not know which path to take. The sons of Salih, perceiving sinuous fibres of mist, claim to have seen signs of a bonfire. Al-Ghatash, however, seeing the tip of a turban buried in the sand, then discovers a buried body, stripped of flesh, with visible canine teeth marks.

"Where there's fire, there are people. This is the body of someone who has died of thirst, and was desecrated by hyenas or jackals."

But the poet of Labwa, instead, went by the indications on the dead man: he noted two deep incisions, parallel, one on either side of the chest.

parameter:

Bin al-Abras

The legendary Abid, known also as bin al-Abras, was one of the youngest poets to have his poem considered among the greatest works of the Age of Ignorance. He was also, undoubtedly, the most infamous poet of them all.

Abid (or perhaps Ubayd – for they are names that are written the same way), although born rich, had been taken from his parents at a young age – as they had contracted leprosy and lived in isolation in a leper colony, on the outskirts of Bostra. The monicker *bin al-Abras* simply means "son of a leper".

As if this weren't already curse enough, Ubayd (or Abid) was supposed to have become intoxicated beyond his limits during a night of betting and greediness, and had laid down in the tent of his own sister, whom he then made pregnant.

Their uncles tolerated the incest (Abid was a great poet, and the sister claimed not to have noticed anything because she did not rouse from her deep sleep); and this circulated with embellishments and prerogatives. Nevertheless, the event affected him, so that from then on, he avoided life's seductions and renounced material goods, surviving on handouts, in the manner of his leprous parents, who had been left in the trench in the Bostra desert for those who were plagued.

Wandering from encampment to encampment, living off the hospitality of the tribes, Ubayd set off in the direction of the celebrated al-Hira, an Arab stronghold in the lowlands of Iraq.

At the time of these events, Mundhir the treacherous ruled al-Hira. He belonged to a Christian tribe, but his particular interpretation of Christianity led him to add Day of Consecration of Good and Day of Consecration of Evil to the calendar. The first foreigner on whom he laid eyes, on those days, would receive, respectively, either one thousand pieces of gold and a virgin slave, or the skin of a weasel and a death sentence.

Abid arrived in al-Hira at dawn. The city was completely deserted. When he heard the crowing of a rooster, a man observed him from the castle door.

That man would be Mundhir the treacherous. That day, the Day of Consecration of Evil. The poet would have received the skin of a black weasel and waited an entire day to be sacrificed, tied to the obelisk that symbolised the inverse of the Cross.

Ubayd's poem is the most solemn, the most melancholy, the most pessimistic of all those 'suspended'. And it shared something with al-Ghatash's poem: deliberate, if not aggressive, irreverence to the genre's conventions.

The classic ode is composed of three fundamental acts: the poet's arrival at the encampment abandoned by the tribe of the woman he loved; his journey in pursuit of her, on horse or camel, when he confronts the dangers of the desert; and the eulogy to the tribe, in which he describes the victories in battle, defeat of the enemy, assembles wise maxims, expounds on his own code of honour or finds an outlet for a typical Arab fanfare in scenes of irresponsible drinking and extravagance.

Bin al-Abras' poem has hardly any of this. Tediously it lists a series of abandoned regions, dwellings that had become lairs for wild animals, places that had become legacies of death, a world where there is dishonour for that which ages.

But there is no traditional invocation of a loved one. Abid mentions not a single woman's name. He even denounces the possibility of love or happiness:

...if encampments move on, people come and go, and there is nothing original, nor marvellous?

If those who inherit will have to bequeath? If those who are taken as ransom are later pillaged?

If he who runs away to see a man return? If he who avoids seeing death never returns?

Man lives a lie, a short period of agony in the machine of death.

Ubayd's ode was a poem dedicated to death. Another eccentricity of this text is the abrupt ending, in the middle of a wild desert scene – the fight between a falcon and a fox.

The great question among scholars who study Abid is to understand the motive, the reason for him having interrupted or ended the poem at the point which, in conventional tradition, would be the middle section. And I have to contend that he had sufficient time to conclude it, between receipt of the black weasel pelt and the moment of execution. I have my own theory.

According to certain medieval biographies, the poet, before leaving for al-Hira, went to the leper colony to see his parents. This occurred at the beginning of the 11th month of the Arab calendar – a sacred month in which murder is prohibited. We know that the Day of Consecration of Evil imposed by Mundhir the treacherous fell during the sixth month. Ubayd would never have taken more than two months to get from Bostra to al-Hira.

The day of his arrival – the day on which he was the first foreigner to be seen by Mundhir the treacherous – fell during the 11th or the 12th month of the ancient calendar. It could only have been the Day of Consecration of Good.

If Abid (or Ubayd) interrupted the composition of the poem it was because he must have received the thousand pieces of gold and the virgin slave. They say that he was a humble youth, detached from riches and pleasures, who opted for a path of abstinence and dedicated his talent to poetry. But I ask: does there exist a man who can renounce life's seductions, for the second time?

ط

toh
16th letter
as a number, 9
in a sequence, the 9th
first letter of طريق, path, and طوف, return

Oh beauty!
Oh women!
Oh deserts!
(Anonymous)

I let my verses echo wherever I went and chose the paths of fury and devastation: Dhu Suyuf's signs were easy to follow. The men of Salih were dead. In front of me, however, the Oasis of Sand.

"I am looking for the route of the sons of Ghurab," I implored, while still mounted on my camel. But I didn't need an answer. Desolate eyes said it all. I got down, reached for the bow in my saddle, unwrapped a twirl of my turban and led my animal to drink, alongside some pits and corrals away from the village.

Arid, the men's faces; but fresh was the water from the well. I decided to wash myself right there, between the bushes, far from the homes that were staked to the ground due to what can only be explained as a lack of courage. It was just before twilight. With a bowed head, I had just finished scrubbing my hair when I thought I heard a raven's caw behind me.

I stood up quickly, imagining it carrying away my sash or my turban in its beak, but the creature had already flown away between the palm trees. When I went to check on my belongings, I sensed a human presence, for a shadow crossed over my face.

Appearing from between the pits and corrals was a woman without a veil, with a black cloak and bow-legged, limping upon encountering me, coming between me and the setting sun, not bothered by the fact that I was still naked.

"Happy is the foreigner who knows not how to read a bird's flight, for within it is written the vanishing of the sons of Ghurab; for within this it is written that nothing endures."

The prophetess ought to have known that not even Layla's footprints had endured. I revealed that I was the poet of the Labwa; and that I was in search of the beauty of that hidden face.

"For this, you need to solve the riddle of Qaf."

And she proceeded to tell me a ridiculous story, of mysterious words written on an amulet, that allowed the past to be viewed. I replied that I didn't know how to read, that I didn't believe in such nonsense, and that I was only interested in Layla's whereabouts.

"In that case, follow the raven's tracks. That is the path of the Ghurab."

I thought that she was mocking me, for a raven leaves no tracks. And I threatened the old woman, who burst into laughter like a bird that bears a bad omen.

I turned my back and spotted a tent where they were making tea. I stopped there to drink, among dirty and toothless men, wearing the tattered rags of those who till the earth.

But the prophetess followed me. With her sharp voice, bringing the admiration of all around upon me, announcing that I was the poet of the Labwa. Later, reading the stars, she described Layla's beauty and narrated my journey in the desert, until the point at which I arrived at that oasis, dismounted from my camel, grabbed the bow from my saddle and took the animal to drink between the pits and corrals where she had been hiding.

She spoke; and sank into the shadows. The next day, I headed in the direction the prophet suggested: she was, without a doubt, that raven.[5]

---

5. *Ghurab* is a word for 'raven', or 'crow'

excursion:

The triangles of Spiridon

It was not completely ignored by the scholars that the theories of the School of Croton, particularly that relating to the right-angled triangle, had a significance that was more metaphysical than mathematical. It is not for nothing that they say a hecatomb had been offered to the gods to acknowledge this tremendous discovery. Personally, I don't believe in that hecatomb, as a historical fact, as its violent and immoderate nature contradicts the School's teachings. But the legend is certainly not accidental and may be related to the doctrine of immortality and of the transmigration of souls, which occurs every hundred years.

It was supposedly Spiridon, born Naim, to the tribe of Labwa, who later adopted a Greek name for having been the first Arab Bedouin to obtain Roman citizenship, having left behind the desert tents to follow the same paths taken by his soul in other lives and former bodies.

Spiridon never gained posthumous fame, but he was a philosopher of reasonable erudition, versed in ancient books, with a keen arithmetic talent. In Alexandria, he came to have free rein over the Library. But he also went to the outskirts, where he descended into the crypts and praised their mysteries. He learned to read from Egyptian papyruses at the same time as dancing naked in front of the ocean and drinking milk from a donkey's teats.

Greedy for knowledge, which he did not disassociate from mystic experimentation, he joined with geometrists who were emigrating to Rhodes, ready to contemplate the perfection of the Colossus and resolve the problem of the quadrature of the circle.

It is necessary here to re-establish a historic truth: it was Spiridon, not Ptolemy, who first offered that the expression $3 + 17/120$ is the value of π. Perhaps he never revealed the finding, for as soon as he obtained it, the possibility of expressing π by any fraction was completely refuted. The number π, the area of a unitary circle, simply did not exist in nature.

This frustration was such that he came to expend his energy in the interminable study of triangles, particularly right-angled triangles. The innumerable geometric properties of these shapes led Spiridon to conceive of them as participants of the circle's divine equilibrium, of which they were but a mundane manifestation.

The theory of reincarnation emerged from there: man was a variable triangular association of material, space and time. The soul, the summation of the angles, in communion with eternity and infinite circularities.

A few disbelievers soon had an irrefutable demonstration of such reasoning, for Spiridon began to recollect objects and people with whom he had coexisted in the past. Initially, he recognised, among the spoils of a rich slave merchant, a crater mixing bowl moulded of silver, with an enigmatic inscription in precious stones that he easily decoded – but it told of his own work when he was Mnesarcos, a Samosian sculptor who had been dead for close to six hundred years.

He then set out for Samos, where he identified, in funerary epigrams, hexameters he had authored when he was Lisias, the mediocre poet of Miletos, deceased some one hundred years earlier.

In Miletos, the face of a prostitute led him to Naxos. From Naxos, he went to Cirene, following the trail of a seal of an archon for whom he had been a servant. There, after interrogating a mule driver, he embarked for Biblos, on the Phoenician coast, and designs on a carpet led him to depart for Jerusalem, in Judea.

The journey was unpleasant. Spiridon was ridiculed by an uncouth grammarian who loved humiliating philosophers.

"I don't believe in any of this, nor do I believe in reincarnation, nor in your capacity to recall past lives."

"But that is a genius of the scholar. Have you heard of the sage of Croton, who first enquired after the history of his own soul and was able to be in two places at once?"

"Rubbish. Primitive legends, as ridiculous as Homer's fantasies."

"No. They are not legends. It is a power that one acquires from the esoteric interpretation of triangles. Each thing, each event, each movement must always be observed from all three of its aspects. The relationship between these – or rather, the triangle they form – defines its metaphysical nature."

"And he who cannot claim to possess a memory of a hundred-year old crater or of the face of a prostitute?"

"I can prove that which I speak of. The crater presented a recurring motif, formed of twelve stones. It was Samos. All works attributed to Mnesarcos possessed similar motifs, always of twelve stones. Or rather, equivalent to the letter μ, the beginning of Mnesarcos, the man who has been gone for six hundred years."

"Mere coincidence. Twelve is a number that appears in all fables: in the labours of Hercules, in the signs of the Zodiac, in that of the gods of Olympus, and even in that of the twelve founding tribes of this Jewish people."

"But not in the figure of the woman of Miletos, whose entire genealogy I have traced…"

"You traced the genealogy of a whore?! Really, Spiridon!"

Spiridon further attempted to seize control of the conversation, reminding him of the fact that he had the pretension of concluding the sage of Croton's incomplete doctrine regarding the most perfect of the right-angled triangles – that with sides of 3, 4, and 5, the only one whose sides make up an uninterrupted sequence and whose perimeter is 12 (a divine number *par excellence*). But they had entered Jerusalem and were overwhelmed by an unruly mob.

"Condemned to die on the cross," an Arab roared.

The grammarian entered a tavern, while Spiridon, seduced by

the people's chatter, left, in the midst of the tumult that followed the men. The narrow, crowded side alleys seemed to augment the suffering of the three criminals who, under the guards' whips, dragged the very crosses from which they were going to hang.

"They are two thieves and an impostor," they heard, in very bad Greek.

Horror fascinates. Sometimes, more so than beauty. This is what Spiridon felt when the procession reached a mount in the city's surrounds. Obscured by the agglomeration in front him, he barely distinguished the noise of the nails being driven and the condemned men's tortured howl. Only after the crosses had been raised could he see them, those outlines of right-angled triangles.

That was the stimulus for an allegorical interpretation. Spiridon surveyed the scene: three people on three crosses, each with four points – 3,3 and 4: therefore, an isosceles triangle with a perimeter of 10 and whose height was less than its base – a symbol of human nature. A height less than the base indicates greater propensity to the earth than to the sky. The value of the perimeter, 10, is twice 5 – which are the outermost points of the human body. The quality of the isosceles, or rather, that of having two equal sides, represents the equilibrium of Good and Evil.

Suddenly, a crash and a penetrating clamour interrupted his thoughts. He looked back, fearfully: the locals were extremely agitated. There was even a woman, aggressive, hysterical, trying to get to the crosses but she was held back by her hair. Spiridon retreated a little, seeking proximity to the Roman guards who were playing dice.

He stayed put, observing the march of death, until he had witnessed the expiration of the last of the three. It was then that he faced the crucified man in the middle. There was something in his face, traces that caused Spiridon to remember something. He observed slowly, attentively, and suddenly an image came to mind. Now there was no doubt. Six hundred years before he had seen that man being born.

"By Allah!" he screamed, in a native tongue. "It's Pythagoras!"

[From the fourth century onwards, Gentile philosophers who converted to the faith of the Roman Empire came to disseminate the version that Spiridon had counted three crosses, four points and (instead of three) five people: two thieves and three divine entities combined in the impostor, which resulted in the perfect right-angled triangle, with sides of 3, 4 and 5 and a perimeter of 12. My sources don't allow for similar chimera. And I do not believe that this improves on the Theorem.]

ي

ya
28th letter
as a number, 10
in a sequence, the 10th
first letter of يمن, right, and يسار, left

Three have the faith:
the Persian, in his horoscope;
the Jew, in his law;
the Arab, in his camel.
(Anonymous)

After having crossed deserts, confronted storms, scaled unstable rock faces and climbed through dark and hidden ravines, al-Ghatash came to stand before the Monastery of the Cave. He must have seen – from atop the precipice that hid the edifice (now demolished) – the fertile valley, the wells of clean water, the small village of monks who bred sheep and grew dates; and – well below, in the cracked wall, a clump of rocks – the rocks that formed a staircase and led to the church's facade, extending into the cavern's interior.

Al-Ghatash must have skirted the ravines in order to descend into the settlement. Signs of the Ghurabs' cruelty were still visible: crosses on top of recent graves; plundered orchards; carcases piled up at the corral entrances.

The son of Labwa probably requested water and a resting place for his camel. But no one responded. The poet certainly insisted, enquired after the direction taken by the Ghurab, and still there was no response. Possibly he addressed himself more than once to half a dozen monks he encountered there and it could not have taken him long to realise that they were all mute.

The poem is somewhat confusing at this point, but it appears that al-Ghatash, irritated, wounded one and dragged another by his hair. Oddly, there was no reaction. For the more that he enquired, the more that he said, the cenobites lowered their eyes, like pigs in a sty searching for peelings.

Al-Ghatash crossed through the silence of the settlement and went in the direction of the church. He climbed the stairs and burst into the temple, now shouting out, slashing with his scimitar at the primitive furniture he came across, as he made his way through the temple. He demanded some information about Layla's tribe. He threatened to destroy everything, unless some human being said something to him.

The section of the church which had been built was spliced to the rock, in such a way that part of it was constructed, part was formed by a natural cavity. This more spacious section narrowed until it ended in a type of throat (where one would presume the altar to be), that continued in a narrow, but fairly tall crack, with many lateral niches, that formed cells at some points. It was in this practically airless and poorly lit corridor that the monastery itself was found.

Inside, four men were working. Each one in his own cavity. They sweated, were dirty and they only lifted their eyes from the vellums when al-Ghatash threw an olive-oil lantern at one of them.

"I'll set the rest of you on fire if you don't tell me where the tribe of Ghurab went. I was with the crippled prophetess. I know they have passed by here."

One of the monks then stamped his feet on the ground, to attract the attention of the others. Al-Ghatash observed an unusual scene: the four conversed in writing, scratching letters in the sand with the point of a staff.

Al-Ghatash was going to grab another lantern when they

seemed to reach a conclusion. Still without talking, the one who had stamped his feet entered one of the cells, placed a few things in a sack and touched al-Ghatash on the arm, pointing to the entrance of the cavern.

Outside, he stopped beside the camel. Al-Ghatash, finally, understood: the mute monk was going to accompany him on the trail of the Ghurab

parameter

Zuhayr

Zuhayr is almost al-Ghatash's perfect antipode. The only thing he has in common is the practice of eating with his right hand. An ancient image says al-Ghatash's life followed the sinuous trail of a serpent; that of Zuhayr, the upright trunk of a palm.

Among Arabs, modesty is vile; and Zuhayr, proud of being from a long line of poets, despised al-Ghatash, who descended from common people: 'The spear is only good when the shaft is good", "The palm tree only prospers if the root is deep" – such are maxims that have origins in Zuhayr's verses.

Zuhayr, a symbol of dignity and prudence, was the only Arab poet not to carry weapons. For the virtue of keeping this pleasure private, he should be seen as a hero.

It is common to attribute the gift of a long life to mythical sages. They say exactly this of Zuhayr. He may have lived to a hundred and twenty years. His Suspended Poem, which celebrates the end of a four decade-long conflict, is an inexhaustible source of wise proverbs:

Destiny kicks like blind camels.
Dissimulate, so as not to be bitten by wild animals, nor crushed by camels.
He who defends not his well with a sword will be without water.
He who rebels against the spear's shaft obeys the tip.

The tongue makes up half of a hero. The heart, the other half.
The rest is no more than a bit of flesh and blood.
How many appear to be worthwhile before opening their
mouths?

It will not take a very attentive reader to sense that the third example is not congruent with Zuhayr's pacifist and conciliatory personality.

The usual – more obvious – explanation is that which attributes, to another poet, this verse, which was subsequently inserted into Zuhayr's poem so as to have the same metre and the same rhyme.

I would like to call attention to the fact that not just the rhyme and metre, but the style is clearly that of Zuhayr. The verse is, therefore, authentic. It just belongs to another poem, long lost, that does not rail against war, but is a kind of *ars amatoria* of the desert, a practical guide to carnal love.

Zuhayr was a great experimenter in this material. His erotic pretences involved more than seven hundred women, of all races, castes and ages. At ninety years-old he was still able to please eleven young wives, simultaneously.

It was Zuhayr who discovered that giving in to a passion is the same thing as losing it. But his theory pointed to an inverse understanding to that of the sublimationist doctrines, such as that of Buddha. He submitted himself to this, as in the case that inspired the opening of the poem, classified as one of the seven masterpieces of the Age of Ignorance.

In it, Zuhayr contemplates the mute remains of Awfa's mother's tents, in the sandy mounds, remembering fine traces of a tattoo; observes the antelopes with big eyes and white gazelles, herd upon herd, alongside the calves that hopped about to suckle. It is at this place that he affirms having stopped, after twenty years, struggling to understand the tracks, as much as he tried.

The scene is a classic one, with which all the poems were expected to open. What catches the attention here is the twenty years. Could it be that Zuhayr would not have had an opportunity, in all that time, to find Awfa's mother, although he knew the tribe's traditional whereabouts, although there were ample fairs where these tribes congregated?

The mystery may be examined in the sequence of the text: Zuhayr calls on a friend to follow the palanquins, which follow the dry beds of seasonal rivers, in the direction of perennial wells; and pass through deserts of white sand, traverse deserts of red sand, hurry to the cool of the oases: and there, alongside the blue waters of an overflowing lake, they come to a halt to let down the women, who dive in, naked.

It was this friend, and not Zuhayr, who had accompanied the migration of the tribe of Awfa's mother. Awfa's mother – they say – always delayed the departure, in the hope that Zuhayr would catch up. But Zuhayr used every strategy possible to arrive at the encampment many years later.

But he always kept abreast of the tales of his companion. This individual, notwithstanding, whose name has not been preserved by history, did not possess the talent to describe Awfa's mother with the precision of the poets.

Zuhayr, in love with Awfa's mother as no one had ever been in love before, surprised the unwary and, before there was any reaction, he pulled off their veils.

"You are Awfa's mother," he said, and lived for a hundred years.

kaf
22nd letter
as a number, 20
in a sequence, the 11th
first letter of كريم, nobleman, and كلب, dog

Two are the innocent:
the pretty woman;
the armed man.
(Anonymous)

After having crossed vast expanses of sand, after al-Ghatash had stolen a camel for the monk, after having spent seven nights rolled in rugs, a voice in Arabic broke the silence of the desert.

"My name is Macários. I haven't spoken a word in seven years."

The son of Labwa then listened to the story of the young man who had abandoned his parents' house in Damascus, and went in search of voluntary exile in the inhospitable depths of the Monastery of the Cave.

Abba[6] Chacur, the oldest of the eremites, who was one of the cavern church's founders and had established the church with his first adherents, came to treat Macários as a son. Macários was, in

---

6. *Abba*, "father" in Aramaic, was a respectful term used for addressing old monks.

a manner of speaking, *Abba*'s confidant. And it was in this role that he learnt of the great temptation that afflicted him.

Because many years ago, there had been a crippled old prophetess, dressed in black rags, seeking refuge in the monastry. *Abba* Chacur turned her away, after a long time in which he seemed to have been fighting against a great temptation.

Then that raven (to use one of Macários's expressions) predicted *Abba*'s death, reading his footprints in the sand, and incited him to solve the riddle whose solution would send him back in time.

Old *Abba* wrote the text of this riddle on the back of a tablet, which bore on its front a cross in bas-relief. He engraved the words just as he had heard them from the prophetess's mouth, without translating them into the usual languages of the time.

Scholars will deny it, but Arabic was still a language without writing. They do not know that *Abba* Chacur had long been working on the systematisation of an Arabic alphabet, which he never came to divulge.

Abba Chacur solved the riddle. But his horror was such, his remorse so great, that he decided to take upon himself a vow of silence. Macários accompanied him; and the other monks, even without knowing the motive, with all their enquiries going unanswered, also remained mute.

Nevertheless, *Abba* Chacur lived tormented by the mysterious text. He buried the bas-relief in the sand, to try to forget about it, and he began to perfect his alphabet, translating the gospels.

One night, *Abba* Chacur seemed to glimpse a figure of the crippled prophetess. He came out of his cell, quickly, but all he found at the foot of the stairs was one of those desert rats, which had dug up the earth, in the very place where the old cenobite had hidden the tablet.

Abba Chacur succumbed to temptation, once again. And he had long prepared for the experience, constantly silent, involved in complicated calculations, forgetting to eat. However, at the very instant at which the phenomenon had begun, the Ghurab reached the grounds of the monastery.

They claimed not to know of the riddle. They merely wanted the crippled prophetess's whereabouts. Only none of the monks would break the vow of silence.

And *Abba* Chacur, eyes fixed on a point in the sky, unmoving at the top of the church's steps, did not see the arrival of the Ghurab, did not see that they carried torches, did not see them dismount from the panting mares, did not see that they enquired, did not see that they beat even the old people, did not see that they pulled down palm trees, did not see them set fire to the corrals, and did not see the blade of Dhu Suyuf's sabre.

Macários observed the happenings in the same manner as *Abba* Chacur. He was also looking towards that shining point by which the *Abba* seemed to be captivated at the moment of the fatal approach of Dhu Suyuf. He saw, rapidly, the scene repeat itself: he on the step immediately below *Abba*, the arrival of the Ghurab, the flaming torches, the men dismounting their mares, the questions, the elderly beaten up, the torching of the corrals, the fallen palm trees and the blades of Dhu Suyuf's sabres.

The Ghurab went off with *Abba* Chacur's body, as he had done with Bulbul's. What Macários had promised to the other monks of the monastery, discussed in writing in front of al-Ghatash, was to retrieve the body of the beloved old man, to give him a grave, in the depths of the cave.

Al-Ghatash did not need to ask whether, among the objects grabbed by the monk and placed in the sack, there was the tablet that contained the elucidation of the riddle.

excursion:

The shipwreck of Sinbad

Western readers of *The Thousand and One Nights*, particularly those who have leafed through Burton's translation[7], would certainly be well acquainted with the story of the two Sindbads, the navigator and the maritime trader (one of them, Sindbad the trader, depending on the edition, is also called Hindbad). The more erudite might have heard of a third Sinbad, or, more precisely, Sindabad – the Persian prince protagonist of a book that tells the story of his education, in the manner of Xenofonte's *Ciropedia*.

The fourth Sinbad – who is neither Sindbad, nor Sindabad – is the legitimate, the oldest of the four, whose failing was merely in not having a book which recounted his adventures.

Sinbad was the favorite servant of a rich widow who traded in myrrh and incense, until the day he embarked for a port on the Gulf of Oman, en route to the emporia of India.

The winds were not always constant, and Sinbad's ship lost its way, drifting aimlessly over the waves. One by one, the crew was dying. Sinbad survived, for he had hidden a bag of dates from the captain between the unburied bodies, which the pagan religion did not allow to be thrown overboard.

It was shipwrecked, and he was the only survivor, on the coast

---

7. Sir Richard Burton's 1885 translation is one of the most well known in English, but Antoine Galland's French translation predates it by more than a century.

of a lost island in the middle of the ocean. He would never have imagined that the men who would rescue him would speak Arabic.

"We are shipwreck survivors and the sons of shipwreck survivors," one of them said. "We traded one desert for another."

The island was small, but it had everything: rivers with clear water, fruit trees and, although there were no wild animals to hunt, the fish were abundant in the various coves that cut into the coastline. The only thing that Sinbad found strange, when he climbed to the headland where the people lived, was the fact that there were almost no women among them.

"This is a cursed island. We are all condemned. Try not to leave your hut after sunset."

There would be no telling of this story if Sinbad had obeyed. That same day, unable to sleep, he heard strange noises outside. He pulled himself up silently and could just make out a sombre movement of men, who entered and exited a large hut, the highest in the village, situated on the island's summit.

When he awoke the next day, he heard the news:

"They killed two more last night."

Sinbad then knew that the women of the island were being systematically murdered and devoured, always at night, without anyone finding out who the murderer was.

Time passed by and it was always the same thing: a furtive movement around the great hut, at night, and dead women, sometimes completely denuded of flesh, by morning.

But Sinbad never risked going outside, until one night one of the men woke him.

"You can come too. You are one of us now."

When he entered the hut, he saw: the women of the island, the few that remained, were lying down on rough woven mats, visited by men one after the other, indiscriminately, on top of them. Sinbad also took his turn.

His friendliness with the men did not allow him to find out why the women were dying in that manner. But, when the women's numbers had dwindled almost to the point of extinction, not only Sinbad but everyone on the island discovered the reason. Because the women were no longer attacked under the cover of night, but at any time of day. Those women were the final remnants of a vast population; and they were, also, the most ferocious.

Sinbad would never forget the way in which, suddenly, one threw herself against the other, with hair flying, roaring, with only their teeth and nails as weapons, killing and then eating the raw flesh of the defeated, and licking up their blood.

With the ever decreasing number of women, conflict among the men over entering the great hut increased, also became deadly. Sinbad was among the strongest. Because of this, he had the privilege of getting to know, along with the other victors and the pubescent girls still existing in a state of humanity, the last wild-woman, Labwa, sovereign lioness – who devoured without herself being devoured.

While she remained on the island, Labwa had eleven husbands and gave birth to many children, princes and princesses of the future tribe that would bear her name. At the same time, the girls previously spared would bring to light generations of servants.

When the Queen was about to die, she rediscovered the art of shipbuilding and revealed the return route. It was Sinbad who steered them back to the mainland. No one knew exactly how. But they suspect that Labwa, as well as the other women, had kept this secret hidden since the time when the struggle began; since the time when they could have returned and decided to stay, until they knew who, among them, was the most voracious.

ل

lam
23rd letter
as a number, 30
in a sequence, the 12th
first letter of لحم, meat, and لبن, milk

If you don't own it,
steal it.
(Ali Baba)

Once, when I entered an Arabic restaurant on Rua Senhor dos Passos, hungry and penniless, my attention was drawn to an enormous Lebanese man who was eating raw kibbe and telling stories in the style of *The Thousand and One Nights*.

I feigned interest, so as to get closer to the kibbe. I remained there, listening, standing, awaiting my chance. At one point, the man mentioned something about a legendary mountain named Qaf.

I asked him to elaborate on this theme, pretending not to know anything about it, without, however, being distracted from my principal objective. I was in luck: the Lebanese man, taking a piece of Arabic bread, began to explain that – according to a belief of the ancient Bedouins – the Earth was imagined as a circular disc, just like the bread before us. Qaf was an enormous mythical mountain, that surrounded, delimited and maintained the Earth in equilibrium.

I took advantage of the opportunity to sit and take one of the other pieces of bread, while asking if the Lebanese man had heard mention of a genie called Jadah and of his eventual link with the riddle that bore the name of the mountain.

He remarked that he had not heard anything in respect of riddles. He also did not know that the genie was cross-eyed. He had not heard the version that gave Alexander the Great's sword as the reason for his blindness. According to him, the genie had always been blind, in both eyes.

I began, therefore (while I broke bread under the table and stole small pieces of kibbe), to tell stories of people who had been victims of Jadah's testimony, in the desert.

When I asked if he knew why Jadah had been left blind, the Lebanese man fidgeted excitedly and revealed (as if it were a secret) that the genie had some sort of cataracts or glaucoma.

"I know many stories about Jadah." And he continued talking, with a full mouth.

I left shortly after, naturally without paying, and went to take inventory of the Lebanese man's stories. In none of them were there scenes like those of the crippled prophetess or of Macários the monk, who had seen the past while looking at a point in the sky.

The Lebanese man, therefore, did not know how the phenomenon had occurred. The narratives that weaved through my hearing had contained the conventional apparatus of tales of time machines, in which it is the people who travel great distances into the past or future. In *Qafiya* it is the past that is seen again as if it were a film.

But the hypothesis that Jadah was afflicted by glaucoma or cataracts was particularly prolific.

With the stage I had reached in my reconstruction of the *Qafiya*, I shivered at the combination of ideas that occurred to me: that of Jadah's opaque eye at times forming a type of screen on which the film of the past was shown for the prophetess and the monk. The point in the sky that *Abba* Chacur had searched for and that Macários had seen must be in exact harmony with the blind eye, which had not been plucked out by Alexander.

This gave credibility to those episodes of the poem and,

significantly, shed light on a specific function of old Naguib's telescope: locating Jadah's blind eye.

parameter:

Shanfara

There are two important facts shared in the destinies of al-Ghatash and Shanfara. The latter renounced his own tribe, a stance which al-Ghatash would end up sharing. Al-Ghatash's poem, the *Qafiya*, was never integrated on to the roll of the prized poems – the same thing happened with Shanfara's *Lamiya*.

The case of the *Lamiya al-Arab* (the Arabic poem in the letter *l*) is in fact surprising. As in the example of al-Ghatash's poem, Shanfara's poem was also considered a forgery, the work of a tenth-century grammarian, a specialist in pre-Islamic poetry, particularly in the original tribes of Yemen – like that of Shanfara's.

The fact that it does not appear in any of the ancient collections is, indeed, disconcerting. I believe the prejudice against the bandit-poets explains everything.

Shanfara was one of these anti-heroes, exiled from the tribe, chased by men of his own blood, living only by his wit and his daring, with no one to avenge his death.

While still a child, he was captured by the Fahm tribe, visceral enemies of the Azd, the tribe of his parents, who were killed in the episode. One day, as the war between the two seemed to be without end, a man of the Fahm was captured by Azd riders, close relatives of Shanfara. And the poet's future was given as ransom.

Shanfara, still a child, had no memory of these facts; and he was not aware of this story until the day he fell in love with the young Umayma, who had just been promised to one of the tribe's princes.

A spiteful girl – whom Shanfara was afraid of tainting with his menial kisses – ended up revealing the truth: Umayma was a cousin of Shanfara's, who would have preferred marrying him. Indignant, the poet went to question his uncle, to learn why he had never been recognised as a legitimate member of the Azd. The response was an embarrassed silence.

"I will not rest under the sands without first killing one hundred of the sons of Azd, because I was kept as a slave by my own tribe!"

Thus began Shanfara's revenge, and he came to live among the wild animals of the desert. The *Lamiya al-Arab* celebrates this animality.

I have closer relatives: jackals, who do not tire: leopards of lustrous skin, hyenas with thick manes.

They are cousins who don't keep secrets, nor abandon those who commit crimes.

Mountain goats run around me, like virgins dragging long tunics,

and they reach the summit at twilight, at my side, as if I were the man of long horns, heading up the steep slope, with crooked legs.

Shanfara had killed ninety eight, when he was ambushed in the night, during the sacred month, in which war is banned. In the heat of battle, his right hand was amputated, but with an assault of exceptional ferocity he was able to slay one more with his left hand, dispatching ninety nine.

This would be the last human being that he killed, in life. Just before dying, already incapable of reacting to the attacks by the men of Azd, Shanfara recited:

Do not bury me, because you are prohibited from my interment, but be happy, hyenas, at these glad tidings!

When you carry my head – and my head is much of me – the rest of my bones will remain abandoned to the storms,
  I will have no more desires on this earth...

No one linked these verses to the oath of revenge made years before. The body was in fact abandoned in the sand.

When it was already half decomposed, the spiteful young woman passed by the site, spitting, swearing, stomping violently on Shanfara's body. They say that, afterwards, she cried and buried the corpse. But she died from an infection of a wound caused by one of the bandit-poet's bones, which cut open her heel as she stomped on it.

Shanfara completed the one hundred he had vowed.

This is the most impressive example of Shanfara's poetic gift, which rivalled those of prophets and wizards. They came to believe that he was not a man, but a genie who was resistant to Solomon's power. They are idiots, evidently. As a bandit and as a poet, Shanfara knew that love's rules are all too obvious, all too logical, all too predictable for anyone to escape unpunished.

م

meem
24th letter
as a number, 40
in a sequence, the 13th
first letter of مريء, virile, and مر, bitter

Why ask God
if you can buy it at the fair?
(Mundhir the treacherous)

From high atop the Falcon's Nest, among the ruins of an old fortress, I caught sight of the black tents of the sons of Ghurab, pitched in the middle of nowhere like grains of dried-up dung. In my hands I had Macários' sack, which contained the riddle of Qaf. The horizon held the possibility of Layla's beauty, obscured by the veil.

If the crippled prophetess really had uttered the truth, solving the riddle would be enough to unveil that face. I opened the sack and spilled out its contents; there were parchments, hides, the stub of a reed-pen, three or four feathers, a splinter of sharpened rock and a wooden amulet, with a cross carved on one side and an inscription painted on the other.

"Decipher this for me, monk, or I will slit your throat."

And I hurled the amulet at Macários' face. The monk turned it around in his fingers, disappointed.

رأس عل شمس
رجل عل شهر
عين عل عشر
جده عل قف [8]

From the Damascenes who watched his birth, he had assimilated foolishness and cowardice.

"I understand Greek and Aramaic, but I'm not familiar with the alphabet in which this riddle is written. The secret of these symbols was buried with *Abba* Chacur's body."

I was unhappy with myself that I could not read any form of writing and I could not slit the throat of someone who could read two.

"Then I will unveil Layla, even without solving the riddle."

We descended the mountain as if on ostriches. From a distance, I heard the camp's dogs barking. I saw fluttering flags. There were thirty-three men encircling us, with spears like the nipples of women in the cold.

"The sons of Ghurab need not fear the wrath of al-Ghatash. I come willing to reveal the crippled prophetess's whereabouts."

When I dismounted in front of the sheik, I noticed smiling lips.

"I have come to take away Sabah's sister. I am offering four hundred and forty camels, to be handed over in Mecca, during the month of pilgrimage, together with the two hundred and twenty agreed upon for Sabah, along with revealing where the old cripple pursued by the Ghurab can be found."

"Then Sabah's sister will be yours," said al-Muthanni, "when the men of Ghurab, by the trail from your mouth, bring the prophetess to the tribe's tents; when the six hundred and sixty camels are handed over in Mecca, during the month of pilgrimage; when the poet of Labwa wins yet another duel against someone of Layla's choosing."

I didn't quite understand that third condition. The two sisters were being confused. Al-Muthanni perceived my confusion.

---

8. During this time, long vowels were not yet written in Arabic. In modern Arabic we have على instead of عل; عاشر instead of عشر and قاف instead of قف.

"And who," I asked, "is my opponent?"

"That one," said the sheik, pointing at one of the thirty-three who guarded us. I looked and saw a man with two swords in his sash: Dhu Suyuf.

excursion:

The mimetic signs of Nakhl

Cultural historians, more specifically those who study the evolution of writing, are unanimous in attributing the invention of this art to the Sumerians; and the discovery of the alphabet to the Phoenicians.

The superiority of the written alphabet over all the others resides in the reduction of the number of signs necessary to represent the whole vocabulary – which renders obsolete systems such as the Chinese ideographic, the Egyptian pictographic (also called hieroglyphics), and all the syllabaric, of which Sanskrit is an example.

The proof of Phoenician precedence in this domain exists not only in archaeological evidence. It is relatively easy to realise that it is Phoenician letters that provided the model for the genesis of all other alphabets, through two of its oldest descendents: Aramaic (from which modern Hebrew, Arabic and Indian writing systems etc, originated) and Greek, origin of Etruscan graphemes and, later, of the Latin, employed in practically all European languages.

Thanks to this exceptional economy, to this fabulous capacity of representing words by their sound and not by their idea, scholars surmise that the stimulus behind the creation of the written alphabet was practical, the fruit of some commercial or diplomatic need. And rare are those who, in this field, link the development of the alphabet to the phenomenon of religion.

Fools, all of them. The alphabet was conceived by a woman who wanted to imprison time.

It has recently been said that written Phoenician was the origin of all known alphabetic symbols. There is, as always, one exception. For near Nakhl, in the Sinai Desert, some indecipherable inscriptions were discovered, clearly alphabetic in nature, that possess not a single trace of a lineage back to Phoenician letters. Expert opinion usually dates them back to the beginning of the second millennium before Christ, which makes them older than the first Phoenician inscriptions.

In effect, four thousand years ago, Arabs from the tribes of Qadar, Madiyan and Nabat dominated all of the desert region of the Sinai Peninsula. As the transit of caravans heading for Egypt was closed off, Pharaoh sent an ambassador to negotiate with the three Arab matriarchs for the opening of a commercial route.

A pact was sealed by a scribe of the retinue, in hieroglyphics. But, shortly afterwards, rebelling against Pharaoh, following non-compliance with an item in the agreement, the tribes of Qadar and Madiyan ambushed and sacked an enormous Hittite caravan, destined for Memphis. The Nabat refused to participate in the retaliation.

"The Egyptian imprisoned my word. There is no force that could make me break it," was the explanation of Zaynab, the matriarch of the Nabat.

Feeling betrayed, the Qadar and Madiyan went to war with the Nabat and came to expel them from Sinai to the region where they would establish the city of Petra, future capital of the Nabatan realm.

But for Zaynab there had been no betrayal. Having studied Egyptian and Akkadian writing systems, she convinced herself that this was a magical art, which fixed the past in an irreversible manner. It did not take her long to imagine the possibility of capturing not just the past, but her own present, at the very instant of its happening, and stemming the flux of time.

But the existing graphic techniques were very complex, with characters so sophisticated that it was impossible for a scribe to write down a fact at the exact moment of its occurrence. Not to mention the cuneiform, with its awkward wedges and clay slabs that still had to be fired in an oven. Zaynab simplified writing in such a way that she came to invent the alphabet, thus greatly accelerating the art of writing. The Sinaitic inscriptions referred to were created by Zaynab, before she was exiled from the peninsula.

And Zaynab did not stop there. From the 'isolated' writing system (in which letters are not linked to the following one), the matriarch of Nabat evolved to cursive writing. This is the method which the majority of languages adopted and is the most efficient that we know of.

But Zaynab pressed on. She engineered a model in which, written down once only, the letter need not be written again, even when it is repeated in a different word. It is difficult to describe the principle of this revolutionary style – but it is easy to speculate that its speed was vastly superior to the system which we employ.

Zaynab, in this way, was able to imitate facts with writing. After arduous training, that involved the practice of tracing the signs in the sand with a reed, she came to record happenings at the exact instant at which they occurred.

Time, therefore, stopped. The story that followed – of which we are a part – is a fragment of poor quality, despicable, resulting from marginal facts, unworthy of the attention of Zaynab, which escaped being fixed into mimetic letters.

There are those who doubt all of this. But the greatest proof of the existence of the mimetic alphabet is that, today, there is not a single trace of it; there is not any indication, nor any evidence that there was a queen Zaynab, of the Nabat.

ن

nuun
25th letter
as a number, 50
in a sequence, the 14th
first letter of نهر, river, and نهد, breast

> *The atheist's great merit*
> *is not believing in the devil.*
> (The crippled prophetess)

When old Naguib recited the *Qafiya*, he became most emotional (and normally stood up from his rocking chair) during the episode in the dog trench, the second duel between al-Ghatash and Dhu Suyuf, that could have brought the poet one-third of his way to winning Layla.

It all started when the son of the Labwa, after hearing al-Muthanni's conditions, having indicated the exact place where the Ghurab men ought to find the crippled prophetess, requested a resting place for the animals. He was counting a great deal on these people being deceived by the Desert of Mirages and not ever coming to reach the Sand Oasis. And he certainly intended, contrary to the prophetess's prediction, to conquer Layla without solving the riddle of Qaf.

It must have been one of his tricks, because al-Ghatash, taking advantage of the fact that the Ghurab were occupied with the camels' saddles instead of watching over the camels themselves (the distance was too far for horses), circled the encampment, turning directly (on purpose, I believe) towards the middle of the harem.

Poets love coincidences. It was exactly at that moment that, veiled, Layla emerged from her tent, accompanied by various aunts and young cousins.

"Your eyes are black full moons set in the sky of a white night!"

However, crossing in front of Layla, al-Ghatash's vision closed in on Dhu Suyuf's horse.

"Dog, son of a dog!" screamed the poet. And, having barely managed to draw his scimitar, Dhu Suyuf was on the ground, clutching two sabres. Macários ran to avert a tragedy. And the three were encircled by the sons of Ghurab.

"He called Dhu Suyuf a *dog*. Which makes this the duel of the dog trench."

The encounter took place on the Falcon's Nest, in the ruins of the fortress. There was a trench which had been dug in the sand there, its walls lined with stone, where there must have been a prison.

Then, armed with wooden staffs, al-Ghatash and Dhu Suyuf descended into it. They were then each confined to a corner, having to confront eleven dogs that were more or less wild, ferociously taunted before being thrown into the trench and beginning their attack. The victor of the duel would be the one who first killed twice as many animals as his adversary. If they survived the dogs.

The first of the eleven approached al-Ghatash. Almost immediately, two others ran towards Dhu Suyuf. No one knows if he had foreseen the movement or if there was some sort of trickery, but the fact is that the man of the Ghurab, with a sharp kick with the sole of his foot, broke his staff in two.

It was these two halves, with splintered ends forming sharp tips, that Dhu Suyuf's hands raised to shove into the beasts' throats, before the poet of the Labwa had eliminated his second dog.

parameter:

Al-Asha

What similarity could there have been between al-Ghatash and Maymun, son of Qays? The latter, better known by the name of al-Asha, was a myopic poet – blind, according to others – whose talent proved to be so outstanding that just one single verse of his could be worth a hundred camels.

He belonged to the Christian tribe of Bakr and was noted for two further qualities: being unsurpassable in satire; and, invincible in drinking. Al-Asha's grave was a centre of pilgrimage for the drunks of Arabia, who poured wine over the dead poet's tombstone to celebrate his memory.

They say that al-Asha possessed the greatest personal fortune ever known since the time of the queen of Sheba. At a certain time, having lived long enough to be a contemporary of the Prophet, he left with Abu Sufiyan, Muhammad's uncle and enemy. Challenged, he responded that he was going to Medina, where the Muslims had taken refuge, to honour them with one of his poems.

"Their law won't do for al-Asha," said Abu Sufiyan, afraid that the poet's support would contribute to the spread of Islam. "You have to renounce a great many things. Women, for example."

"But, at this point, it is they," said al-Asha, rubbing his wrinkled hands, "who have already renounced me."

"Gambling," insisted the Prophet's uncle.

"I can entertain myself offering my tips to others."

"Wine."

"I can drink water from the well that I reserve for my camels."

Abu Sufiyan looked meaningfully at his companions.

"Tribe of Quraysh, this is al-Asha! Gather together all the camels necessary so that no water is left in the well!"

Al-Asha was capable of making fun of it all. Even of himself. His Suspended Poem is the only one to contain an element of satire in the classic motif of the poet who arrives at his lover's encampment.

I liked her by chance; she liked another who was not me; and he liked another who was not her.

But al-Asha cannot be reduced to just this virtue. His capacity to describe a scene or a shape was as magnificent as it was unique. They say that his severe myopia contributed to this style.

He once compared the advance of Persian hordes, in a battle against the Romans, to nightfall over the earth's expanse; and he was able to distinguish the soldiers, for some wore shining golden earrings like pearls hidden in an oyster's shell, untouched by mud.

They are images in which brilliance and darkness alternate – there are no shapes strictly speaking, there are no profiles, there are no figures. This tendency made al-Asha the first of the Bedouin poets to describe a woman, capable of being recognised with one's eyes closed.

Under the shade of long hair, face resplendent as a mirror, she walks like a gazelle with wounded hooves over mud;

you perceive her retreat from the sound of bracelets and necklaces, like rustling shrubs, protesting against the wind;

not a single garden with untended slopes, replete with green grass, where heavy clouds release their copious burden,

the day will come with perfume like that of hers wafting; nor will it be more beautiful when the sun sets.

Verses such as this must indeed come from a myopic. The

woman alluded to was Hurayra. I gathered a vague notion of her beauty when I studied other poets, who described her in a more precise manner, more geometrical, more natural. Even dishevelled and unadorned, when in mourning, she caused men to keel over when she appeared from her tent.

Al-Asha also keeled over. But it so happened that al-Asha was blind. However, only a blind man like al-Asha could have sensed something in her that was not just proportion or form.

siin
12th letter
as a number, 60
in a sequence, the 15th
first letter of سن, tooth, and سيف, sword

There are four pleasures:
to laugh, to eat, to love
and to understand.
(al-Ghatash)

The cheats who considered me beaten had yet to experience the might of the son of the Labwa. I will roar like a lion attacking a herd of gazelles. I will kill like a lion bringing down its paw on a wild ass's rump. The Ghurab will come to eat the hyenas' feast, and al-Ghatash will unveil Layla's hidden face.

Leaving the Falcon's Nest, I walked through the desert bearing with me the monk and the riddle. The tribes cheered me as if welcoming a Persian prince. Wild animals hid from me as if fleeing charging elephants. Until we arrived at Yathrib, where we were welcomed by a stray dog.[9]

I went clearing a path through the streets. In the marketplaces, Macários drenched himself in wine with pimento and almost

---

9. Yathrib is the ancient name of Medina, the sacred city of Islam.

plunged into a lamb stew. I preferred to admire the dancers. I had sworn not to rinse my mouth, nor wash my body; not to use perfume, nor musk; to eat just dates and drink only water – for as long as I did not possess Layla's beauty.

In front of the synagogue of Yathrib, Macários stopped me.

"This is a temple of the sons of Israel. There are men of science here."

Abdurab was the old man who showed him in. Macários carried the sack, with inscribed scrolls and *Abba* Chacur's tablet. But Abdurab, rabbi of Yathrib, also did not know how to read the symbols.

"Then find someone who can!"

I said this to Macários, who shook with fear, as I pulled the sack from him and threw the parchments out on to the street. Macários wanted to save them, trying to hold my arm.

"Don't do that! They are from the book of Matthew translated by *Abba!*"

I restrained myself from hitting him; and pushed him against a donkey.

"I will be waiting at the al-Qubá Gate, on the side farthest from the city. But I will not be the one to chase the man who tries to leave without the riddle. It will be arrows that go in my place."

I returned eleven days later. I suspected that the Ghurab had headed straight for Mecca and was in a hurry. Macários was nowhere to be found. My only alternative was to try the synagogue.

Abdurab was much thinner and much older. But he had deciphered the tablet. Macários, who looked like a skeleton, was drawing letters on a sheep skin, next to the dog that had accompanied us since our entrance to the city.

"I deciphered all of it, up to the last word. But I don't understand what it means."

It was Macários who recited the riddle to me. I, too, did not understand it, as usually occurs with the caste of those who should first be understood.

Abdurab refused my golden dinar. I did not seek another way to thank him. In one of his deep eyes, I saw that he carried the burden of a monk; in the other, that he had worked with the pleasure of one who does the impossible.

I left the temple and went to saddle my camel. On the desert trail, I passed by the encampment of the tribe of Salih, ever more eager for Ghurab blood. A woman, with tattoos on her hands and face, half covered by her tent, maliciously flashed her teeth at me. I looked upon the girl's happiness with despair.

The pleasures were fourfold. Only Layla would be able to provide me with the last one. I pulled Macários by the arm:

"Let's go. There must be wise men in the desert who still know how to solve riddles."

excursion:

The woman who divided by zero

Being a people of poets, it is only natural that Arabs were great mathematicians. Even during the pre-Islamic period, they had accumulated a vast understanding of astronomy, indispensable to navigation in the desert. They must have been responsible for other inventions: they created trigonometry; they practically discovered algebra; and they developed the most important mathematical concept – that of the number zero. I can affirm that this conquest can be attributed to just two people, one of them being the famous al-Kwarizmi.

But there are no books that tell the story of Malika, daughter of Mansur, son of Sarjun, descendent of the Labwa on the maternal side, born and educated in Damascus, who wove, cooked, rode, shot arrows, played the lute, recited all the poets, executed the dance of the seven veils, spoke and wrote in seven languages and calculated with such perfection that she was not celebrated exactly for this reason.

History tells – or so the legend goes – that everything began in 658 AD, during a game of chess played in the governor's palace, in Damascus, where Malika's father, an orthodox Christian, held the position as secretary for new Muslim chiefs.

The players were the two greatest of the time: the Armenian Hagop and the Jew Zeev. Four wise men attended the game and each bet twelve golden dinar. The first one expected a white victory, in the one hundred and first round; the second, a black victory, in the one hundred and second round; the third, also a black victory, but in the one hundred and third round; and the fourth, for the whites, in the one hundred and fourth round.

Suddenly, Malika burst in from behind all of them, affirming that checkmate would be played by the blacks, in the one hundred and fifth round; and threw the exact sum of twelve golden dinar on the ground – which now meant that the pile held a pot of sixty coins.

The four sages, the governor, the other onlookers laughed a great deal at this juvenile insolence. But the game did end in the one hundred and fifth round, with victory going to the whites. When the four sages bent over to count their twelve dinar – as none of them had actually predicted the outcome – Malika quickly claimed the sum.

"The sixty dinar belong to me and I can easily demonstrate this."

"You bet on the black, and it was the white that won."

"The facts are not quite like that," Malika said. "At the start of the game, the five gamblers each held twelve dinar. This was the case up until the hundredth round. After the one hundred and first, one of the sages had lost the bet; and the four remaining gamblers had fifteen dinar each. After the one hundred and second round, three gamblers each came to have twenty dinar. At the end of the one hundred and third, myself and one of the sages each had thirty dinar. When this sage erred in the outcome of the hundred and fourth round, I came to have the whole sixty dinar."

There was some discussion, and Malika appeared to concede the argument that no one had won the bet.

"If no one won, we should then divide sixty by zero: $60 \div 0 = 0$. The sixty dinar belong to no one."

At Mansur's suggestion, the governor would hold on to the dinar that belonged to no one and distribute it among the poor. But Malika was not happy for long. She realised that there had been an error in her calculations. In effect, $60 \div 0$ was 0, just as $6 \div 0$ was 0, just as $600 \div 0$ was 0. If you apply basic mathematical principles, 0^2 would be equal to 60, or to 6, or to 600, or to any other number – which was absurd.

That was when Malika declared that any number divided by zero was equal to itself, so that dividing by zero is the same as not dividing at all.

Malika's torment began exactly at this moment, for she realised that any number divided by one also equalled the number itself. Zero and one were, therefore, the same number. It was therefore the same thing to believe in a single God or in no god at all.

So that they would not kill her, Mansur ordered her locked up, in her house. This did not prevent her, by way of the servants who looked after her, from spreading new heresies, such as the one that negated the authenticity of the miracle of the dividing of the loaves.

Malika stopped believing in fractions, in truth. For her, the universe was only composed of whole numbers. Fractions were not really numbers, but merely expressions of relative size. When one says half a loaf, what is meant is a loaf that is half the size of another. In this way, a loaf of bread divided by two results not in half a loaf of bread but in two pieces of bread – and one piece of bread is still bread. Division, therefore, is multiplication; and vice-versa.

Christ certainly broke the loaves. The miracle was in the generosity, not in the magic of multiplication.

It might seem that we digress from the theme of dividing by 0, but that is not the case. In truth, Malika soon realised that this theory was only valid for numerators equal to one. But this train of thought was fundamental in returning her attention to the general problem of the arithmetic of fractions.

There was a property that caught her attention: the asymmetry between numerator and denominator. The value of fractions grew in relation to the increase of the former and decrease of the latter; and shrunk, if the inverse was the case.

From this it would result that: firstly, if the numerator were zero, the fraction will have the smallest value possible – or rather, zero; secondly, if the denominator were zero, the value obtained will be the greatest possible – or rather, it would correspond to the greatest quantity of countable things existing in the universe.[10] In a word, the Final Number.

---

10. According to atomists, this number is the sum of atoms of all bodies, animate and inanimate, present at the Final Judgment.

She wilted, grew old, became sick, stubbornly confronted all the hardships imposed by her father, in the attempt to calculate the Final Number. She realised that incommensurably large numbers presented a series of distortions – in the same way as the very small (like 1, for example, that is neither even nor odd; or 2, prime and even, whose double is equal to its square; and 3, prime consecutive to another prime etc.)

But she continued, discovering ever larger quantities; and was approaching the Final when, on a sinister night, while working in her dark and grim cell, dishevelled by the cold wind and whipped by the sand that came in through chinks in the narrow doorway, she could not endure the horrifying aberrations of those gigantic numbers, and died.

Mansur did not consider himself guilty. And he was not. It was the Large Numbers that had killed his daughter: because they were indivisible by 1; because their root was identical to its square; because, if consecutive, they remained odd numbers: and, if added, they became smaller.

ع

'ayn
18th letter
as a number, 70
in a sequence, the 16th
first letter of علم, wisdom, and عشوة, darkness

I love the concept of the woman, just the one.
This one, her, that one, that other one;
who will show me the difference?
(Imru al-Qays)

My greatest contribution to the study of *Qafiya al-Qaf* was surely that of having succeeded in reconstructing the reasoning of the rabbi of Yathrib.

Like the majority of Arabs of that era, Abdurab did not know how to read or write in that language. As a rabbi, he certainly had a command of Hebrew. He therefore must have had a notion of the similarity between these languages.

When Abdurab was holed up with Macários in the synagogue, he only had access to the parchments and tablet. These bore the Arabic version of Matthew, in the same unknown symbols of the riddle.

It cannot have been difficult for a man used to dealing with manuscripts to discover that this script comprised twenty-eight letters. But this wouldn't have meant anything if Abdurab had not noticed that these same characters were sometimes written in isolation, preceding lines or groups of lines. Or rather, that the isolated letters also functioned as numeric symbols and served to number the text's chapters – conforming precisely to rabinical usage.[11]

By virtue of being a rabbi, for believing in each letter's inherent numerical value, for believing that any alphabet's order obeys a transcendental law, Abdurab concluded that the first chapter of the Arabic text was numbered with a sign corresponding to the first Hebrew letter, and so on successively.

Put in a sequence in which they appear in the parchments, twenty-two of the twenty-eight unknown symbols had equivalents in the alphabet of Israel. It was sufficient, therefore, to transcribe the tablet into Hebrew symbols:

ראס על שמס
רגל על שהר
עין על עשר
גדה על קף

It was now possible to understand a good part of the text:

...over...
foot over Moon
eye over ten
limit over...

Three words had no possible reading. But Abdurab knew from the similarity between Hebrew and Arabic; that often the sound of the letter *samekh* (ס) is confused with the sound of *shin* (שׁ). And they are each used in, *salaam* and *shalom*; *Mussa* and *Mosheh*; *qud* and *qodesh*[12].

---

11. Coincidentally, the gospel of Saint Matthew includes twenty-eight chapters, the number of letters in the Arabic alphabet. The Greek alphabet has twenty four letters. It is also not coincidental that the *Iliad* contains exactly twenty-four cantos.
12. Respectively, 'peace', 'Moses' and 'Sanctity'.

One just need substitute the *samekh* with the *shin* to obtain:

ראש על שמש

or rather:

head over Sun

The last word was missing. It was not, for certain, a Hebrew term. But the rabbi was able to pronounce it as "Qaf" – the name of the imaginary mountain, obtaining therefore *limit over Qaf*, which makes sense, for pagan Arabs did think that that mountain delimited the Earth.

Abdurab had arrived at a final interpretation. But, as he had just finished writing "Qaf", he remembered that "limit" (גדה), pronounced *gadah*, was also the Hebrew way of saying the name "Jadah", as with the example of "camel", said *gamal* in Hebrew and *jamal* in Arabic.

He must have hesitated momentarily. They were both about Qaf. He opted for the solution that seemed to him more congruous with an incantation of idolaters:

head over Sun
foot over Moon
eye over ten
Jadah over Qaf.

parameter:

Alqama

As with al-Ghatash, Alqama was never exactly famous. Of him, of his life, of his work, there is nothing known that could be considered authentic, apart from some poems (whose beauty, it is necessary to say, amazes) and one solitary episode, linked to the "Day of Halima", one of the most tragic in Arabic history.

On the Day of Halima, the tribe of Ghassan, ally of Byzantium, warred with the tribe of Lakhm, ally of Persia, whose sheik would be executed for treason. Halima was the virgin daughter of the lord of Ghassan, to whom the Byzantine emperor granted the title of monarch. Known for her magic arts, the girl would anoint the bodies of the greatest warriors of her father's army with a perfume that brought them good luck. On Halima Day, she perfumed a hundred of the thousand warriors.

The monarch won; the sheik allied to the Persians was decapitated. But the only casualties of the victorious army were ninety-nine of the hundred anointed by Halima. The hundredth of these, Magid, took one of Alqama's brothers captive.

Coincidence or not, Magid was daring enough, during the ritual that preceded the battle, to pull Halima to him and kiss her on the mouth, leaving on the girl's lips the mark of his teeth.

She had complained to her father, who so enjoyed the scene that he promised her to Magid, if he should return alive. It is at this point that the legend takes obscure twists and turns.

Gossipmongers had affirmed that Halima had received a stranger in her tent; and that, as she was no longer a virgin, her arts no longer had any effect.

This suspicion was shown to be true when Magid abandoned Halima on the dawn of her wedding night, under the pretext of an obligation to avenge the ninety-nine dead hanging over him. He died as well, of course, because no one escapes death twice.

Halima still had not found a second husband when Alqama (known also as "the stallion", for having won a duel of virility against Imru al-Qays) presented himself to the lord of the Ghassan. He came with the proposition of rescuing his brother, held hostage, from the hands of the powerful monarch. But he had no money – or rather – he was not generous. It was then that he conceived his greatest verses.

In them, he speaks vaguely of a woman who smells strongly of saffron that lingers in the air even after the camels have departed, of a crazy man who tries to follow a track over a stone floor, of a tunic that was tight at the hips, of a docile gazelle reared in a stable.

At this point, Alqama begins to talk of his mare: solid as a rock which the current tumbles down the bed of a flowing river, a dromedary's lips, coated with green malva, dribbling down its chin. And he compared it to an ostrich searching for the hatchling from its eggs in the desert. And the poem continues, growing with wise maxims, a tavern scene and a new description of his bravery and of his skill on horseback.

The monarch paid particular attention to a passage in which a rider travels through inconstant deserts, frightening, crossing the undulations at night, along trails as intertwined as a spider's web, oriented by the mountains that were but shells of abandoned boats, and by protruding bones that broke through the skin of unburied corpses.

The final verses were a snare: they praised the generosity of Halima's father's, calling attention to the one who recited them – an enemy, who had travelled there, alone.

The monarch, wanting to live up to his reputation in the poem, freed Alqama's brother. But the poet, from that day on, was never to be seen again. And Halima was given to one of her father's servants, liberated some hours earlier.

It seems that the monarch knew his own desert well and thought that the mountains were like shells of shipwrecked boats, and he was used to seeing corpses whose white bones broke through their decomposing skin. He knew where Halima was by the scent of saffron, even after the camels had departed. He quite admired the poet Alqama's mare, hard like the rocks that rolled in the deep river and fast like the ostrich in search of its young.

No one understood how the sheik of the Ghassan discovered that it had been Alqama, the stallion, who had invaded Halima's tent and caused the death of ninety-nine heroes. I, in his place, would have come to the same conclusion.

They are complete nonsense, the arguments attesting that there was no proof; that it could have been any other poet; that every desert is the same, each mare the same, every woman the same.

Alqama never became completely famous: he never missed an opportunity to humiliate a king.

fa
20th letter
as a number, 80
in a sequence, the 17th
first letter of فقير, poor, and فاض, free

True wise men
never find happiness.
(Al-Ghatash)

In Mecca, during the month of pilgrimage, the law of peace was held sacred. Even so, I kept my sword in its sheath, strapped to my shoulder. I could not trust in the honour of the cousins of men I had killed.

The tribes had journeyed to the great Black Stone. I passed by tents of arrow-makers, vendors of anise liqueur, tattoo artists with their quills and pots of henna, preparers of lotions based on camel urine, carders of wool, blacksmiths, and weavers, merchants of saddles, arrows, rugs, perfume and spices.

I entered Mecca, without having drunk, and unwashed. The streets were simply impassable. Macários was lost in the confusion of people enraptured by the tellers of fables.

"A son of Labwa should not enter Mecca. It is a city of pagans."

An idiot, that monk. But I had no time to reply.

"Where, dog of the dogs of Labwa, are the six hundred and sixty camels?"

They were men of Ghurab, who awaited Sabah and Layla's bride price. I looked at each one in turn, but did not see my cousins. Salih had also not entered Mecca, out of the same reverence as Macários. I had my sword strapped to my shoulder-bag. But it was the month of pilgrimage.

Without responding to the insult, I continued on my way to the Black Stone. It would not be easy to get to. The barrier of humans was dense. I felt pity for the beasts that would be sacrificed. I was able to break through a group of Bedouins who were sacrificing eleven white camels. It was only then that I remembered I had nothing to offer at the Stone.

I quickly turned my head, searching for Macários, who had a stash of dates with him. I could not see through the incense smoke and I had to abandon the shrine, going against the flow of the multitude of pilgrims.

I caught sight of Macários an hour later, almost at the city limits. Standing next to him was a man who seemed to be meditating, staring at the sky.

"This is Abu Hilal, counsellor to the princes of Yemen. He has the gift of being able to read the stars. And he ate all the dates in your sack."

"Dog, son of a bitch!" I held my sword against the wise man's chest. At that moment, however, lions' roars echoed through the desert. It was the tribe of Labwa that was entering Mecca. In a blink of the eye, I counted six hundred and sixty camels. The first of the three conditions had been met.

excursion:

The Phoenician sphere

The longest war in the history of the universe lasted exactly four hundred years. Naturally, it was a war between Arabs, which involved practically all tribes; and it would be exhausting to try to list them, so often did they divide themselves to switch from one side to the other.

We know only that – if it is not a legend – it must have occurred between the sixth and second centuries before Christ; and that it was sparked by ownership of the Phoenician sphere.

A notable work of artistry, this sphere. They say it was exhumed from the tomb of King Hiram of Tiro, friend of Solomon, and it had been wrought by a Yemeni sage, a member of the embassy of the queen of Sheba in Israel.

It comprised a compact metallic globe on whose surface was carved, with admirable precision, a map of the world as it was then known as well as the countries that were yet to be discovered.

Enveloping the metallic globe, concentric with it, there was another globe, made of crystal; and between these, a dense layer of a colourless liquid whose composition was obscure, in which tiny granules of metallic powder floated. Examined from close up, these grains were revealed to be miniscule figures, innumerable, but confined to twenty two different forms, copying the twenty two letters of the Phoenician alphabet.

The sphere's secret lay in these tiny little metallic letters. It was stated above that they floated in this dense liquid. It was not exactly like this: they were all actually constantly and randomly spinning, at high speed, changing direction and course at any instant, and colliding against each other, which made them change trajectory and embark on a new collision course, infinitely.

Physicists today would argue that the energy lost in these collisions would gradually lead to the cessation of movement. It would be true, if we had not been dealing with Phoenicians.

The sphere was, however, the only human design to realise the ideal of perpetual motion, the permanent and incessant working of a machine, with no other source of energy apart from its own motion. But this was not the motive that brought the desert tribes to desire it.

So, he who fixed on a specific point on the world map represented on the globe would see these tiny little metallic letters pass by, which would formulate words, phrases, whole sentences, a book of infinite stories, like *The Thousand and One Nights*.

No one knows if it was King Solomon, Hiram himself, the queen of Sheba or a Yemeni scholar who first noticed that the story told by the tiny letters for each point on the map corresponded, precisely, to the facts of what was occurring in that place, at the moment of observation.

If any reader, paragraphs before, thought the existence of a complete world map during Hiram's time to be implausible, you now have your answer: the very narratives told by the letters revealed that which existed on each point of the Earth's surface.

The sphere was initially stolen by a group of Bedouins led by a certain Assad, an ancestor of al-Ghatash, who, imagining that he could establish a mathematical formula to predict the trajectory of each of the letters, wished to be able to calculate and know the future of each point on the planet.

But it was not long before they were attacked by Arabs of diverse clans who, based on the same principle, sought to discover which prior movement caused the current trajectory of each tiny letter, and so on and so forth until arriving at the initial impetus, the first letter set in motion, therefore, the origin of the universe.

For four hundred years, the sphere passed from one band to another, successively, without them being able to discover the formula. In one of these skirmishes, it was lost, buried in the sand, somewhere in the deserts of Arabia.

The end of the conflict coincided with the appearance of an ascetic sect of infinitists, who – with no time to worship an interminable number of gods – had little interest in readings of the future and past, and proclaimed the Phoenician sphere to be the Book, incessant, incomplete, imperfect, that bore not a single revelation, that reached not a single conclusion, whose only redeeming feature was that, in an assembly of infinite gods, at least one will have granted you forgiveness.

saad
14th letter
as a number, 90
in a sequence, the 18th
first letter of صخر, stone, and صحراء, desert

Just to state the obvious
it would be necessary to read a thousand books.
(Malika, who divided by zero)

I waited for the last ray of sun to sink into the Red Sea before putting the dagger back in my waistband. I fastened my turban over my face, just like the thieves of Babylon, and followed the musky scent of Layla's hair.

Quartered camels still attract dogs. I didn't hear any barking when I reached the Ghurab encampment. Serpents would not be so cunning; nor would rats be so keen; nor scorpions, so lethal: Layla's tent rose in front of me.

My dagger silently brushed over strands of her braided hair. Among rich carpets, ebony trunks, golden lamps, perfume betrayed Layla's presence to me. I decided to pull back the colourful curtains that separated me from her desireable face. However, when they fell to the ground, there was Dhu Suyuf:

"You fell right into our trap, dog of Labwa! You will have to defeat me in a new challenge!"

To avoid violating the sacred month, the tribes decided on a duel of words. The victor would be the one who formulated a question that a wise man among wise men could not answer. I looked and saw: it was Abu Hilal, with his belly full on my dates, the wise man among wise men.

"What is Qaf?" I began.

"The circular mountain that surrounds the Earth, which no one has seen nor touched."

"Who is Jadah?"

"A gigantic genie, whose only eye was blind and who once leaped over Qaf."

"What is Jadah's power?"

"To come from the past to bear witness against men."

I was interrupted to give Dhu Suyuf his turn.

"Who is the most beautiful of women?"

"The one whom you don't know."

"What is the love that never dies?"

"The one that doesn't consume you."

"What is needed to defend love and beauty."

"Your sabre and your right hand."

Dhu Suyuf then grabbed his sabre with his left hand. One of the tribe's camels had no time to bellow. I did not see if it was its head that jumped from its body; or its body that dispensed with its head.

parameter:

Amru bin Kulthum

Not even al-Ghatash came to be as vain as Amru bin Kulthum, in whom two great lineages of poets converged. Amru certainly attributed his glory to such ancestry, as one does with the good racehorses. But no one would remember him if it were not for an old camel.

The plot contained four actors: Sarab, the camel; al-Basus, the camel's owner; Jassas, al-Basus' nephew, of the Bakr clan, of the Christian Wail tribe; and Kulayb, of the Taghlib clan, sheik of Wail.

The Bakr and Taghlib often still shared the same encampments, when al-Basus tied Sarab to a stake, in front of Jassas' tent. But Sarab freed herself, attracted by the handsome camels of the Kulayb herd, and went to join them.

Now, Kulayb did not recognise the camel belonging to al-Basus – who was of the Tamin tribe – and he tried to kill it, but the arrow only struck the animal's full udder.

Groaning in pain, leaving a trail of blood and milk behind her, Sarab returned to Jassas' tent.

"Shame on Bakr! Is this the treatment deserving of guests of the sons of Wail?!"

Faced with al-Basus' disgust, violated of his right to hospitality, Jassas went to demand an explanation, following the trail of milk and blood. It did not take him long to discover the culprit, whom he saw coming after the injured camel. The two argued, of course. The sheik was alone. Jassas thrust a spear into Kulayb's chest, in exchange for the camel's injury.

They say that it was a forty-year war. According to my calculations, it could have lasted close to four hundred. During this period, peace was attempted innumerable times; and innumerable times the ancient hate resurfaced.

It was during one of these truces, ready to be broken, that elders from both clans of Wail decided to seek an arbitrator for the conflict – arbitration which fell to the most powerful Arab prince of the time: Amru bin Hind.

Bin Hind then demanded that he receive two ambassadors, one from each clan. But, instead of through argument, he would decide on the basis of who recited the more beautiful poem, improvising, with the same metre and the same rhyme.

Amru bin Kulthum was sent as the Taghlib ambassador. It was he who recited first. The audience shivered in front of such arrogance.

This is because the poet, finger in the air, would pull out his enemies arms as one picks thorns from a cactus: would throw heroes' skulls to the ground as loads fall off camels; would drink from wells of clean water while the tribes cooled themselves off over mud marshes; and instead of captives and plunder, would return from war with kings threaded on a spit.

All of this was said in front of the prince. Some of the more attentive observers noted, however, a strange fact: bin Hind maintained an air of amusement (some would say derision), from the beginning of the poem and even while listening to the arrogance of the Taghlib envoy.

The poem began with an exhortation to a certain "mother of Amru", who had tarried in serving him, in the tent he had gone to with friends, to surprise her, half-naked, with pale arms, immaculate, with the feet of a long-necked camel that had not yet given birth: the smooth and full breasts like vaults of ivory; and a lean and lissom body, steady over heavy hips and fleshy calves.

Still today they discuss who this "mother of Amru" could have been – whether it was the poet's own mother, victim of an incestuous passion; whether a servant in a tavern, where the scene of debauchery was played out; or whether she was one of his cousins, who left with the camels when the grazing dwindled.

None of these hypotheses provide an explanation for bin Hind's smile. It is just that few are those who understood the subtlety and power of the insult: bin Hind was also known as Amru.

ق

qaf
21st letter
as a number, 100
in a sequence, the 19th
first letter of قدر, destiny, and قبلة, direction

Ask the dead
if they desire peace!
(Tarafa)

Between the scene in which al-Ghatash lost the duel of wisdom against Dhu Suyuf and the following one, in which Abu Hilal began to conceive of the instruments that would allow the experience of returning to the past, there is a lacuna, verses that have been lost in the process of oral transmission.

Unfortunately, the missing passage is that which reveals the riddle of Qaf. The dissenters consider this omission to be evidence of its inauthenticity. I believe just the opposite: if the poem were inauthentic the imposter would never have left out the solution to the riddle.

The concrete fact is that Abu Hilal, who had the gift of reading the stars, accomplished the extraordinary deed of interpreting the mysterious text that *Abba* Chacur had recorded. It was not quite as hard for me to reconstruct this reasoning, from the starting point of certain relatively obvious facts.

1st step: Abu Hilal, initially, isolated the text's nouns, forming a kind of matrix:

head	Sun
foot	Moon
eye	ten
Jadah	Qaf

2nd step: he realised that he could classify these nouns in two subsets, that of the things that are over (1st column) and that of the things that are under (2nd column). Each of these subsets also allows subdivision: that of common nouns (from the 1st to the 3rd line) and that of proper nouns (4th line).

3rd step: the scholar noted that the group on the left, from the 1st to the 3rd line, shared the same nature – they were names of body parts. The subsets on the right and above the same line would have to follow the same rule. Therefore, *Sun* and *Moon* are celestial bodies; and Abu Hilal was an astrologist. He had profound knowledge of astrological terminology. It would not have been difficult for him to realise that *ten* was also an element of the horoscope. In this context, it could only refer to the *Tenth House* or more precisely to its vertex – identified by the term *mid-sky*, the position of the Sun at astronomical midday.

4th step: Abu Hilal noted that the subset of body parts were to Jadah as parts were to a whole. As such, the celestial elements *Sun*, *Moon* and *Tenth House* should also be contained in Qaf. The mountain of Qaf was, therefore, in the sky. The mountain of Qaf that encircles the Earth and keeps it stable – that which no one sees nor touches – was none other than the great imaginary circle of the constellations of the Zodiac, traversed by the seven heavenly bodies and by the twelve houses.

5th step: Jadah was above Qaf: Jadah was above the Zodiac. Enter, then, Macários. The monk must have told the scholar the experience of the *Abba*, who turned not in the direction of the Sun or the Moon, but sought a precise point in the sky. In the language of riddles, *head* can signify "first" and *foot*, "last". The Tenth House was found in the middle. His eye would have fallen upon it.

6th step: Macários, once again. We know that the monk assisted in the work of deciphering with Rabbi Abdurab. We also know that he copied letters on a sheepskin – and we can presume that they were characters of the riddle, its numeric value and the translation of the text. It is not absurd to suppose that he had revealed the method employed by the rabbi to Abu Hilal. Although the astrologer could not read Arabic, it was not difficult for him, with the help of Macários, to recognise in the symbols that formed the word "Jadah" (which is written with just the three consonants J-D-H) the numeric equivalents of 3, 4, and 5. To place Jadah over Qaf was to divide the Zodiac in sections proportionate to the numbers of its name. The horoscope was complete, with the graphic solution to the riddle of Qaf:

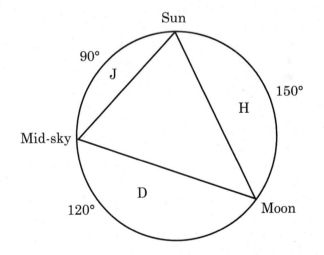

excursion:

Ali Baba's cave

It is not certain whether the systematic thinking, to which the Greeks gave the name philosophy, was first employed in the desert. But since remote times, Bedouins had spent much effort on a rational understanding of the universe, influenced by learned writings of the ancient world – such as the *Book of Ptah Hotep, The Wisdom of Ahiqar*, and *The Book of Proverbs*.

Precisely because Arabic is such an eminently poetic idiom, such force should be recognised. It is given a lot less merit by those who think in modern German, and who thought in classical Greek or ancient Tupi – languages in which two distinct people understand the same sentence in an identical manner.

From the seventh century on, after the conquest of the Levant by Muslim forces, Arab philosophy came to be, essentially, theology: either Islamic or Christian. Censorship by the caliphs at this time was very efficient; and many profane thinkers were condemned to watch their books burned or to have their own bodies separated from their heads.

For this reason, a group of wise men went into exile in the Lebanese mountains. They comprised forty-one individuals: six Sunnis, three Shia, twelve Druze, five Orthodox, thirteen Maronites and two Monophysites. They defended the thesis that clemency was incompatible with justice, therefore only the guilty could be subject to forgiveness. Hence all sacred texts would be false, for they presented God as a being simultaneously just and compassionate.

In the cave where they sought refuge, they were never discovered. There was no police force with sufficient manpower for the capture of forty one philosophers.

The rift, as always, came from within. One of them, named Ali Baba, insisted that the others come round to admitting the possibility of the existence of God, opting exclusively for the virtue of justice or of clemency.

We still do not know which of the two Ali Baba chose for himself. But there remains no doubt that he ended up revealing the cave's password to the caliph's guards.

"Open, sesame!" they shouted from outside; and the forty philosophers were captured, trussed up and boiled in oil, poured into the wineskins in which they were trussed up.

It is not very difficult to see in this tale the story of *Ali Baba and the Forty Thieves*. And it is not by chance that it was never a part of the old Arab manuscripts of *The Thousand and One Nights*, having appeared for the first time in the famous French translation by Antoine Galland, in 1705, who had first heard it among the stories of the Maronite Hana, of Alepo – a city close to the mountains where the episode of the forty-one philosophers took place.

Whether or not Galland's narrative is false, whether or not there was shared identity between the two Ali Babas, the fact is that the tradition introduced by the forty-one remained at Mount Lebanon. For some time, the sultans of Lebanon had to persecute one or another wise man accused of heresy and atheism.

Around the eighteenth century, influenced by the circumstances of the verb *to be*, which in Arabic, is only conjugated in the past, the so-called "Beirut School" determined that the condition of "existing" is achieved exclusively with death.

The evolution of thought stemming from this principle rendered itself so exact that it came to comprise an absolute understanding of existence.

The final step was taken by the philosopher Dawud (or David, as they say in English), who had been born in Brazil, descendant of Lebanese immigrants and in whom flowed the blood of Labwa.

He was perhaps the greatest human mind. Among his accomplishments, that of having proposed an exact solution for all metaphysical problems.

The collection of his thoughts, entitled *The Dialogue of Things*, is considered to be a work of philosophical excellence, the ultimate treatise, the perfect book. So perfect, that it can never be written.

ر

raa
10th letter
as a number, 200
in a sequence, the 20th
first letter of رَأْس, head, and رجل, foot

Realising of desires
is work for the stupid.
(Aladdin)

In truth it was a blacksmith in Mecca who, following Abu Hilal's plan, invented, in addition to the mariner's quadrant and the astrolabe, the device that guided a journey through time.

It consisted of a graduated circle representing the orbit of the sun and the twelve signs of the Zodiac. From the centre of the circle, there rose a perpendicular shaft, around which two pointers rotated. The first of them indicated the position of the Sun and should have been moving at the rate of one degree each day. The other – which marked the position of the Moon – advanced 13 degrees automatically, with the displacement of the solar pointer.

Notwithstanding the fact that the instrument needed to be recalibrated at least every three months, to correct distortions, it was possible to identify with relative precision, the day and time at which the Sun and Moon reached a position in relation to each other of 150 degrees.

In this event, it was sufficient to verify, with the other available instruments, if the mid-sky (where the apex of the tenth house falls) formed angles of 90 and 120 degrees, respectively, with the two heavenly bodies.

Abu Hilal instructed Macários in the handling of these apparatuses, teaching him to recognise the signs of the Zodiac and to perform the calculations that would allow him to determine the apex of the twelve houses.

At the appropriate day and time (more or less two days after the full moon, close to twilight), when the same celestial configuration would repeat itself, the scholar walked to the middle of the desert, accompanied by the monk, al-Ghatash, three camels and the dog that Macários had adopted in Yathrib.

The Sun was already fairly low when they had the camels settle down in an area of the desert where there were stone outcrops. Al-Ghatash accompanied Abu Hilal with his measurements, which the monk verified. As the exact configuration of the three points would occur one degree of longitude further east, the eye of Jadah would be seen with a certain imperfection and for a brief period.

But al-Ghatash was disturbed by Macários' dog, who would not stop growling.

"It seems like galloping horses," he said, noting a faint movement on the horizon.

"I don't think so," came the voice of the monk, who abandoned the instruments. "The dog is barking in the direction of the rocks."

"Jackals!"

He spoke and reached for the bow tied to his saddle, but the shot went awry because the camels had been frightened, fleeing for all they were worth.

In the meantime, four jackals emerged from between the rocks. Al-Ghatash had no choice but to brandish his sabre against the most daring, while Macários was controlling the mounts.

Wounded on the snout, one animal retreated. A second jackal was also hit, this time fatally; and the others fled.

But the eye of Jadah had already disappeared. Only Abu Hilal, impassive as wise men are, could see the retreat of time: the retreat of the camels, the manipulation of the quadrant and of the astrolabe, al-Ghatash's disquiet, Macários' movement and the barking of the dogs.

parameter:

Harith bin Hilliza[13]

Bin Hind, then, summoned the ambassador of the Bakr clan. Harith bin Hilliza arrived, with a long tunic that swept the ground, with sleeves so long they reached the middle of his fingers. His face and head were covered in a turban, exposing only two intelligent eyes. For Harith was, in his time, the most intelligent man of the Bakr.

The audience cleared a path. Harith interpreted this movement as the reverence that was naturally his due. He was mistaken: the news had already spread that he had contracted leprosy.

The ode followed the classic norm. Harith evoked the love of Asma and of a certain Hind – which stirred rumours about the poet's intimacy with the prince's mother.[14]

Hind lit the fire in your eyes, revealing a refuge in sublime havens...

Harith, of course, did not sink to Amru's insulting level. Bin Hind understood this. He paid ever more attention to the image the poet had created of the camel, whose feet, at a gallop, raised more dust than a sandstorm.

---

13. This passage should not be read before that of the parameter "Amru bin Kulthum".
14. Bin Hind means "son of Hind".

The poem's sequence consisted of no more than a eulogy to Bin Hind, the attack on the Taghlib, and the enumeration of the virtues and victories of the sons of Bakr.

The people who gazed upon us went blind, faced with our large neck, our broad disdain;
death shrouds us as one who wants to stone the mountain's summit, covered with snow, parting clouds,
soaring over time...

When Harith ended the poem, he was certain of having won. Curiously, no one noted the slightest sign of approval from Bin Hind. On the contrary, someone even commented that it was with disdain that the prince dismissed him.

The Bakr and the Taghlib, besides the innumerable Arabs from other tribes who watched the duel, gathered in the vicinity of Bin Hind, who came to announce the winner.

"I wish to give the poets that which they deserve. I am not able to tell Amru that he has won. I am not able to tell Harith that he was worse."

Joy for the Bakr, frustration for the Taghlib. Popular opinion was waiting precisely on a result such as this: Amru had abused his arrogance, in contrast to Harith bin Hilliza's moderation and diplomacy.

In the midst of the commotion that Bin Hind's announcement provoked, a few noticed Harith retreat, timid and obscured under his tunic and turban. And they were not even interested in Amru's fanfare, which incited the Taghlib to a new war.

The poets knew very well who had truly won. Who was Prince bin Hind to tell a despotic and conceited man like Amru that he was better? How could Prince bin Hind tell the truth to a liar like Harith, whose leprosy would never allow him to mount a camel or to have women whose names were Hind?

shin
13th letter
as a number, 300
in a sequence, the 21st
first letter of شاعر, poet, and شيطان, demon

I have never pardoned:
I have not the pretence
to possess a virtue
attributed to God.
(Dhu Suyuf)

It would not be this time that I would see the eye of Jadah. At the memory of Layla, a great hatred rose up in me and I ran to destroy the instruments that Abu Hilal had hung from the camel's saddle. But I restrained myself. The throng that I had detected on the horizon was now quite clear.

"We are from the tribe of Qudra and we are searching for our cousin Khalil, kidnapped by bandits who fled in this direction."

Not one of the three of us had seen anything. Pensive, one of the sons of Qudra dismounted from his horse and began to walk around, observing the ground. It did not take him long to notice the spots of blood from the jackal.

That was when an owl soared past and landed on one of the

rocks. I predicted that they would take the bird to be Khalil's soul, which had come to seek revenge.

"Someone has died here who has yet to be avenged!"

Macários wanted to conduct a sermon about the superstitions of paganism. I was more practical.

"The owl has not yet hooted," I said, taking an attitude of someone who was ready for anything. But it was not my lucky day.

"*Isquni! Isquni!*" [15] hooted the bird, giving the sons of Qudra the proof they had lacked.

"Someone has died here who has yet to be avenged!"

He repeated it; and ran for the rocks, recovering Khalil's body with ease.

In fact, it was Khalil of the Qudra, who had been among the rocky outcrops, in the jackal's den. The body, bound hand and foot, was lacerated and had bite marks. The animals had already disemboweled the body and must have been eating the viscera when we attacked them.

I believe it must have been Macários who noted that there were no signs of knife wounds, nor of arrows. But the four horsemen turned against the only armed man.

"When the prohibition of the sacred months has ended, Labwa blood will be spilt to compensate for that of Khalil."

"I'm not ashamed to kill. But I do not draw my sabre for just any reason."

And I performed the gesture, proving that I would confront the four. Macários swore to my innocence and invoked the testimony of the sage. The sons of Qudra kept their eyes fixed on my sabre.

"It is blood."

Macários ran to look for the dead jackal, that I had disposed of a great distance away. However, with a fabulous thundering, in the midst of a strong wind that raised sand over our heads, an immense figure hid the sky with its spectre of fire without smoke.

In spite of the sand, I made a superhuman effort to see Jadah and that horrendous, deformed face, with one empty eye socket and one opaque eye. From within that rough and suffocating

---

15. "Give me a drink! Give me a drink!"

throat, I heard the bellowing voice as terrifying as the growling of beasts in the depths of the caves:

"The blame is on al-Ghatash. Khalil came mounted on a camel abandoned by al-Ghatash among bandits, so old that it could not run when attacked by jackals."[16]

---

16. Consult chapter ن, page 45.

excursion:

The trial of Abdallah

One of the many characteristics that Arabs share with other Semitic peoples is a passion for judges. In Israel, the great kings were judges. Hammurabi, a Bedouin who ascended to the Akkadian throne, was famous only because he had established a Code of Law. Ahiqar, the Aramaic scholar, was a counsellor of justice in the court of the Syrian emperor.

Among the desert tribes, the first laws were founded on the principle of compensation: *an eye for an eye, a tooth for a tooth* was a maxim that was propagated throughout the Middle East. With the passage of time, such asperity was tempered, giving rise to the concept of indemnity. Even so, practising justice continued to be the seeking of revenge for the aggrieved.

Some Arab scholars, meanwhile, having established that the punishment of a guilty man did not prevent the appearance of new criminals, developed a theory that a penalty should only be applied so as to prevent a subsequent offence. As such, the punishment of simple thieves came to be heavier than that of murders of passion – because the former generally disregard the law; the latter, do not.

This thesis also underwent an alternative development, among the tribes of the desert. Considering that the purpose of justice was to prevent crime, and not to avenge it, sheiks and judges came to punish only potential crimes, people who could possibly come to commit them.

Such was the misfortune of Abdallah, a great horseman and one of the greatest archers of the Labwa, who was possibly the father of the poet al-Ghatash.

Abdallah had once returned from a hunt, to the tents pitched in the surroundings of Palmira. He rode a black stallion, which dragged a gazelle that had yet to be disembowelled, and from his quiver only one arrow was missing

Patriarchs from various clans approached sneakily, accompanied by many men, all armed, to see him dismount. Abdallah, his back turned, neither saw nor spoke with anyone, occupied in loosening his Damascene sword from his saddle.

Because he had neither seen nor spoken, he could not have known that his cousin Rizqallah's dog had spent the whole night barking throughout the encampment, and that the animal's tracks appeared, intermingled with human footprints, from next to the tent of Jalila, his wife, future mother of al-Ghatash, who had arisen early with an excess of perfume in her hair; and neither that the first order given to the servant by Rizqallah (another possible father of al-Ghatash) was to wash the turban and tunic to be worn until that evening.

The men who saw Abdallah's movements that morning had no doubt as to the natural order of the facts and they pronounced their accusation, loudly.

Abdallah still had time to jump on the horse's back and shoot, while the arrow shot by Rizqallah resonated against the tempered iron of the Damascene sword.

From this day on, Abdallah, guilty of a capital crime, no longer had any rest. He was once imprisoned in Damascus, at the request of the sheik of the Labwa, but he was able to bribe the Byzantine guards and escaped. Recaptured by the Kalb tribe, on the way from Homs, he again managed to escape, making use of a knife he carried under his turban. He achieved a further two or three spectacular escapes, until Rizqallah himself captured him, when he left Baalbek, disguised among fanatic pagans who accompanied the procession of Adonis.

The trial of Abdallah brought together all the clans of the Labwa and people of the most diverse tribes, in addition to the most notable judges of the time. Nevertheless, contrary to what you may think, they were not all in favour of condemnation.

They initially discussed if it had in fact been demonstrated that Abdallah would have killed Rizqallah. Those prosecuting the case were categorical: Abdallah was born of a noble lineage, casually wielded the Damascene sword and had come with the natural excitement of a hunt, where he had used only a single arrow.

Things began to get complicated when the judges demanded proof that the dog's barking and Jalila's perfumes had the reach that they wished to ascribe to them. It was easy to make the dog bark again, but the essential oils used by Jalila on the eve of the crime had already been whisked away by the wind.

The accusers came to hold the advantage again when Jalila herself confessed that she had lain down with Rizqallah as well, although she could not say from which of the two she had become pregnant.

From this point on, the legal debates reach their highest level in Bedouin history. The first question is with regard to the identity of the accused: it was necessary to ensure that the Abdallah who arrived from the hunt was the same person who stood there in front of the judges. There were unanimous testimonies from all the tribe, but no one was able to demonstrate that a person stayed the same with the passage of time.

Nothing had been resolved, and there arose the hypothesis that the true criminal was the master of Damascus who had forged the sword. But the objection collapsed when they remembered that Abdallah still had arrows in his quiver.

In the end, Fuad, the oldest and wisest of the judges, demanded a demonstration that the word crime had the meaning of "crime", and not any other. It was perhaps the most complex phase of the process. In fact, no one was able to demonstrate that not only *crime*, but any other word had the meaning that was attributed to it.

"This is nothing more than a mere convention," shouted Fuad, with his arms in the air.

It is clear that the sheiks of Labwa did not accept the final decision, and resolved to take justice into their own hands. Only that, in the midst of the tumult, taking advantage of the confusion he had caused in the court, Abdallah escaped, once again.

ت

ta
3rd letter
as a number, 400
in a sequence, the 22nd
first letter of تبر, gold, and تمر, date

*Nothing is so grandiose
that it deserves to be taken seriously.*
(Al-Asha)

The character of Macários the monk deserves a slight digression. The *Qafiya al-Qaf* gives us a figure who is not very honourable, somewhat subordinate, a far cry from the actual heights to which Macários historically must have reached. He was a man familiar with books (we saw how he quickly commanded the Hebrew and Arabic alphabets, as well as the principles of numerology by means of letters); he possessed a great capacity for observation and logical reasoning (we know that he easily learnt the basics of science from Abu Hilal); and he possessed a fine poetic sensibility.

The monk, at this point, had learned the poet's verses by heart and it was a matter of reciting them, in the hope of one day learning how to perform them.

This shatters a false paradox, raised by the 'inauthenticists', which holds that the poem's final lines could never be known, considering that the poet dies at the exact instant that he finishes composing it.[17]

Now, it is evident that al-Ghatash (like every Arab poet in the Age of Ignorance) possessed his own *rawi*, or his "reciter" – a person who knows not just the master's poems by heart, but also knows the circumstances that were involved in the composition, being able to comment on them.

Macários was at al-Ghatash's side up until the last moment; he was the *rawi* of the poet whom he followed; and the poems he recited on the streets of Najran were those cultivated by the son of Labwa.

After the cycle of adventures that I have already revealed to you, al-Ghatash and Macários entered Najran, in whose vicinity Layla's tribe was encamped. We are now in the last day of the sacred month of *Muharram*. The Ghurab was continuing to flee from Salih, who drew nearer, constantly growing stronger, swelled by the best men of the Kalb, Udhra, Tanukh, Bahra, Tayy, Ghassan, Jusham.

Two nights earlier, the full moon had appeared. At twilight of that day, the celestial conformation that reveals the eye of Jadah would occur again. In Najran, someone was awaiting this moment: Macários the monk.

Al-Ghatash was in the middle of a game, among Bedouins, who sacrifice camels whose remains – after being quartered – are won by drawing straws, using arrows.

Macários withdraws. He goes outside the city, searching for the best position from which to observe the sky. It was purely astrological criteria that led him to the Ghurab tents.

The monk approaches the Ghurab encampment. The men of the tribe had let their guard down, taking advantage of that last day of peace. Suddenly, Macários sees al-Muthanni's standard flutter and remembers, with the remorse of one who failed to fulfill a promise, the vow he had taken in the Monastery of the Cave: to recover *Abba* Chacur's body from the tent that sheltered those sinister spoils of war.

---

17. The verses of the *Qafiya* were composed in such a way that al-Ghatash lived the events narrated in the poem.

Macários goes into the encampment. He is fairly close to the desiccated corpses of the *Abba* and of sheik Bulbul. He knows that he will not manage anything alone. And it is the hour of the phenomenon. He stops, looking towards the sky, at the exact point.

Just then, some of the girls of Ghurab emerge from between the tents. They are unveiled. Layla is among them and it is she who screams, warning of the invasion. Macários, at a loss, calls out, like one shouting for help, when men appear.

"Al-Ghatash! Where did you go?"

parameter:

Tarafa

The similarities between al-Ghatash and Tarafa are, above all, formal. The former's verbal aggression results directly from his character, while on the other hand Tarafa's virulence is merely rhetorical.

Tarafa was the only case of a poet – a great poet at that – who did not inspire admiration from his relatives. Born in the Christian tribe of Bakr bin Wail, he was orphaned while young and was raised by his parents' siblings, who squandered a large part of his mother's inheritance.

As an adult, he could have laid claim to his rights, but he was, essentially, a hedonist. He lived a life of decadence, among drunkards, singers, gamblers. Although he had not received the education that his lineage took as a given, he came to excel as a poet.

But Tarafa was not respected. He ended up expelled from tribal living and had no other alternative than to mount a camel and live by pillaging.

You, who criticise me for loving war and adoring wine, can you grant me immortality?

Let me drink, then, until I am sated. If we die tomorrow, you will see which of us will be thirstier.

There is a curious aspect to Tarafa's life: no one remembers ever having seen him with women, although the poet referred to them (especially to their shapely legs) as one of the pleasures of existence, in addition to wine and the horse. His classic poem – also classified as one of the 'suspended' – opens with mention of a certain Khawla, who many have identified as a youth of the tribe of Kalb, but who was never seen in Tarafa's company.

Over a floor of rocks, the traces of Khawla's encampment shine like the remains of a tattoo on the back of a hand.

It is not known exactly why, but, shortly after he was banished, one of Tarafa's cousins resolved to give him a second chance, bringing him once more into the tents of Bakr bin Wail. There, he was treated little better than a servant, charged with caring for his cousin's camel herd.

Evidently, Tarafa did not stop drinking; and in one of these great binges he ended up letting the camels escape. And he had to flee, sentenced to death, through all the deserts, until he found the hospitality of the princes of al-Hira.

It was in this court that Tarafa finished the poem that would be lauded as one of the seven best. The Arabs of al-Hira were impressed by the fact that one third of the verses were dedicated to the poet's camel, whose beauty few before him had managed to capture.

She has thighs so perfect like a palace's lofty portico;
the furrows of the whip on her sides are trenches in the smooth face of a rocky hill;
her eyes are hidden mirrors in a cave – and the sockets of stone are two pools of a spring;
and she drags her tail as a slave would, showing to her master the hem of a long white skirt.

But it is not known what intrigue Tarafa's cousin hatched, such that the poet and the one uncle who remained loyal to him received from the prince of al-Hira the mission of taking a letter to the governor of Bahrain.

During the journey, the uncle asked that a young traveller read the contents of the missive. It was, as he had suspected, a death sentence. Tarafa, a model of loyalty, refused to turn back. He continued alone.

The governor granted him the favour of allowing him to choose the method by which he would die.

"Fill me to overflowing with wine and then bleed me from the depths of my intestines."

Conforming to Bedouin custom, Tarafa's camel was tied fast next to the grave. The legend tells of strange facts: in the first place, the stones on the grave appeared at dawn on the third day to have been removed. The camel had freed itself from the ropes. Tarafa's body had disappeared.

A witness swore that he had seen the camel free, over the open grave, trying to put its dry teats to the corpse's lips. As Tarafa had died with ropes tied to his two arms, stretched out horizontally, forming a cross, there was no delay in the heresies that Tarafa was the second incarnation of Christ.

It was the poet's wicked cousin who contradicted them.

"Impossible. Tarafa was a thief. The camel he rode was mine and her name was Khawla. He stole her when he allowed the others to escape."

No one paid much attention to the implications of this pronouncement, but I want to highlight the third verse of Tarafa's poem:

At dawn, the palanquins left, taking with them my sweetheart, like ships drifting down a riverbed.

The first interpretation, the usual, is that the poet was lamenting the departure of a cousin, probably the same Khawla. But why could it not be a lament for the camel's departure?

ث

tha
4th letter
as a number, 500
in a sequence, the 23rd
first letter of ثَار, revenge, and ثمَت, price

> *You don't kill a pig*
> *without sweetening the knife*
> (Anonymous)

In fact, as the girls of Ghurab could testify, it had not been al-Ghatash who had been in the encampment and caught a glimpse of Sabah's sister without her veils. The Bedouins who had been gambling with the poet also bore witness in his favour. But Dhu Suyuf demanded reparation, a duel, with the despairing clamour of the monk as his proof.

"No one calls for someone who is half an hour away."

Al-Ghatash, who would not cease in swearing of his innocence, suddenly changed his tone:

"I accept the challenge. As long as I have the right to choose the weapons this time."

Dhu Suyuf agreed to the Labwa poet's conditions; and this defined the terms of the duel that would earn him dishonour, banishment from the tribe and of being forgotten by Arabs.

"The victor will be the one who recites the greatest number of

175

verses in praise of Layla, in the rhyme of *lam*, like that of her name, and in long metre, like her figure."

A murmur of indignation burst out from the Ghurab, a tribe in which no one any longer composed verses; but it was already too late. The next day, the people of Najran gathered to watch the dispute.

No one doubted that al-Ghatash would be victorious. But the Ghurab, together in force, maintained the advantage of pride. Some Labwa men also attended, among them one of the poet's uncles, the only one not to stand looking at his own feet.

Dhu Suyuf began to recite. Tradition has not preserved any of these verses: they were correct; but were without beauty. He had already recited from memory those he was able to recall from tribal tradition and embellished them through improvisation, which proved no more than coarse variations of the originals.

He was quite exhausted when he reached a hundred. He coughed. He tried to resume the thread of his narrative, but he presented the one hundred and first verse in a different rhyme.

It was al-Ghatash's turn. The people of Najran stood in awe of the fluency of his rhythm, at the delicacy of the metaphors. Calmly, he had already completed ninety-nine verses of unsurpassable perfection when, suddenly, a number of armed men burst in, encircling the few members of the Labwa tribe.

"This is for the blood of Khalil!"

It was the Qudra, in a fury of vengeance. Al-Ghatash, however, did not react, as one would expect of an Arab poet. On the contrary, he recited the one hundredth verse while watching his relatives fall.

"Shame on the Labwa!" screamed al-Ghatash's uncle, lying flat on the ground, with his face in the dirt and his neck under the blade of a sabre.

He still tried to turn his neck to see if the tribe's poet had drawn his bow or his sword, but he did not live to hear the one hundred and first verse of his sister's son and to watch the unhindered flight of his murderers.

Al-Ghatash won the duel. He had fulfilled the second of the three conditions to obtain Layla. And he was condemned never again to rest under a Labwa tent.

excursion:

The story of Aladdin

Arabic literature (and in particular the Arabic narrative) is, fundamentally, geometric. More than telling a story, the primitive narrators of the desert intended to sketch a picture. It is not by chance that among the Arabs calligraphy is practically the only decorative art.

The book of *The Thousand and One Nights* does not deviate from this principle. It was the first human attempt to represent the infinite. The version we know (first translated in the West by the erudite Frenchman Antoine Galland) is just a fragmented image of the original, written under the nefarious influence of the Persian book *A Thousand Nights*, that has nothing of the infinite and was centered around a certain Scheherazade, woman of flesh and bone.

The true Scheherazade was, and still is, a female genie. The genies of Bedouin mythology have little in common with those beings imprisoned in lamps or sealed chests. They were bodiless entities, passing through material states, situated between gods and mortals, dominating inhospitable regions, where they accosted solitary travellers, driving men crazy and inspiring poets.

There are too many to count, like, for example, Dalhan – a cannibal who appears in the form of a man mounted on a black camel; Ghaddar, who entertains himself torturing prisoners;

Hatif, invisible, who gives imprudent advice; Shaytan, who reigns over flames; Ifrit, who assumes animal forms; Shiqq, who has one arm and one leg, half a body and half a head; Ghul and Qutrub, who prostitute themselves to men and women, respectively; Silat, who makes people dance; Sut, who makes them lie; and Scheherazade or, more accurately, Shahrazad, who, perversely, satisfies desires.

Shahrazad would usually rise out of the Bedouins' tents to incite them to reveal what they had dreamt. The cases speak for themselves: Nabil wanted to be the richest man alive and was subsequently exiled in the desert, without the ability to leave, owner of an inexhaustible well of clear water. Fatima wished to be the most loved of all women and stirred the libido of four hundred men, all lepers, who chased her through the streets of Damascus. But the tragedy of Harb was the most memorable: yearning for immortality, he was buried alive and still screams today, from the depths of the grave.

Genies were always fought against. The first to defeat them was the extinct god al-Uzza, when he imprisoned a great many of them behind the circle of Qaf mountain, which encircles the Earth.

Of those that escaped, four hundred and twenty were later captured by King Solomon, who entranced them with the power of a magic ring.

Few genies remained free. Shahrazad was one of them. She persisted, in her horrendous destiny, in perverting men's ambitions, until entering the tent of a young Bedouin storyteller of the Labwa tribe, whose name was Aladdin.

"I want to know all the stories possible," was the answer to the seduction of Shahrazad.

She laughed at the naivety of Aladdin, who – for as long as he lived – would never have time to listen to all the stories engendered by the human spirit.

Shahrazad saw that Aladdin had lit a lamp and had sat down on a mat, to listen. The female genie began to narrate. The lamp's flame went out. Aladdin relit it countless times. The Labwa tribe left, and he stubbornly remained, in the tent, listening to Shahrazad's narrative.

And he aged, still listening to the "genie's" fables; until he died. Shahrazad had won. She had known that Aladdin would not live long enough to hear all the stories.

It just took her a while to realise that she, too, had fallen into a trap the young Bedouin had set for her.

For Aladdin knew that every narrative leads to another; and that, to another; and another; and so on, successively, until the first comes around to be told again and the process repeats itself, infinitely. In truth, the possible stories are finite, but none is the first; nor the last.

Like the circle of Qaf mountain, like the circle of Solomon's ring, the stories that Aladdin wanted to know had also formed a circle. Shahrazad was imprisoned in this circle, which is, in essence, the symbol of infinity.

The original *Thousand and One Nights* tried to reproduce Shahrazad's work. It is not coincidental that the character of Aladdin from the corrupted version that reached us is a youth who gains power over a genie.

Today, the true Aladdin is no more than a handful of bones buried in the desert. Next to him, Shahrazad remains enslaved, unable to finish an infinite chain of stories that takes turn after turn and never reaches an end; and that, at heart, is more than just a single story.

خ

kha
7th letter
as a number, 600
in a sequence, the 24th
first letter of خالد, eternal, and خال, void

I love the tribe of the bats,
for among them
every female is beautiful.
(al-Ghatash)

I reined in my camel to contemplate Hyena Mountain. It was almost erect like a young woman's bosom, falling a bit to the side, like that of one who breast feeds for the first time. I reached it soon after and I climbed up the path with the gentlest incline.

In one of the burrows dug into the side, an oryx calf called out and leapt around its mother's corpse. He no longer had any family lineage, like myself. The difference is that I was still capable of establishing another.

Macários carried the small animal, seeing that the last of my arrows had struck it in the neck. He became our meal that night, roasted with no spices over bare rocks. His mother's flesh still had not begun to smell, but we could already hear the hyenas that inhabited that infamous place.

Even so, I fell asleep. I dreamed of the unveiled face of Layla, who kissed me on the mouth, like a lioness who licks the navel of the newly born, when the barking of Macários' dog woke me. It was not quite Layla, but the stinking, horrifying hyena, that was licking me on the lips.

With my dagger, I attacked the wild animal, which fled to a hiding-place nearby. I ran in pursuit of it, searching the darkness. The hyena was not where I had imagined it to be. Instead of it, I touched the thin, tattered and repellent figure of the crippled prophetess, smiling like a crow that had soared in from the Inferno.

"Damn!"

And I threw myself, catching the old woman under the weight of my body.

"I am going to take her to the Ghurab, to fulfill the third condition!"

"But remember al-Muthanni's words: *when men of Ghurab, by the trail from your mouth, bring the prophetess to the tribe's tents. If I am taken by your hands, it is Dhu Suyuf who wins.*"

Damn those who are right! I resolved to free her, after holding her quietly a little longer under my body. She dissolved in the night like a pebble thrown into the abyss.

"How can you be attracted by such a deformed body?"

I responded to Macários saying that I had no other means of taking a scrap from the old woman's cloak.

"Your dog sniffed out the whereabouts of the crippled prophetess."

parameter:

Urwa

Urwa was, essentially, a thief. This emphasis may seem strange, yet one of the principal occupations of well-born men, among the Bedouins, was to pillage enemy tribes.

But there was a significant difference: Urwa did not steal for himself, but to distribute indiscriminately among criminals and the destitute.

In the mountain caves, he came to establish a community of outlaws who lived off what Urwa stole. Few committed crimes like he did.

Arabs consider themselves to be a generous people. The right to hospitality is sacred among them. Each chief of a group of tents is morally obliged to protect whomsoever requests refuge, even if that person is a mortal enemy.

But such demonstrations of generosity were undertaken on a personal basis; and such people were not disinterested. Urwa was the first to conceive of it as an anonymous, independent virtue.

"I am not, like the hermits, a man to eat alone," he said, stealing a verse from Hatim al-Tay.

Urwa liked to compare himself to sacrificed and quartered camels, whose pieces were bet on by means of arrows. To display his wealth and nonchalance, he supplied whole herds for this type of game.

And when merchants of Syrian wine adorned their tents and

raised their standards, when servants from all the tribes were sent to help in refilling the enormous wineskins made of camel skin, Urwa plundered the entire stock, to give the drink away for free.

In the famous verses that recount the crime, all copied from other poets, one notes an immense contempt for the weak, for the man who goes on his haunches, at night, searching for bones from the encampments of others, or for the one who is happy and stretches out a hand when he sees someone milking a camel

The story refers to another famously generous man: Hatim al-Tay, whose verses Urwa took pleasure in stealing. They say that he was a great gentleman, whose kindness reduced him to misery. From his wealthy past he retained just one black mare, the fastest animal that had ever sped through the desert, which he kissed on the mouth on his nights of loneliness.

One day, the richest among the Arab sheiks went looking for Hatim al-Tay. He did not immediately declare the reason behind his visit; and he waited a few hours for the meal.

He thought the meat a bit tough, and was surprised at the vast quantities of it, because Hatim had not gone beyond being a beggar.

"I came here to buy the mare," the sheik burped, thus concluding the dinner.

"I would be able to offer it to you for free; if it hadn't already been in your stomach."

Urwa knew of this story; and he wanted to steal it from Hatim al-Tay. He began to rid himself of everything, from the more insignificant objects to the ones he held most dear – which included an Indian scimitar, forged by the best blacksmiths of the Punjab.

Nevertheless, he continued having to steal in order to support his vast multitude of vagabonds. One day, seeing the scimitar at a fair in Palmira, he slaughtered the old man who was selling it, stabbing him with a dagger, also stolen.

This incident led Urwa to lose his sanity. Because the beneficiaries of his munificence transformed immediately into the targets of his looting.

It was in this period that he composed what is perhaps his only authentic verse:

The true bandit is the one whose face shines, and spreads the fear of death among the men he encounters.

Then, at the prime of his insanity Urwa decided to exterminate all of humanity and finish off the institution of ownership, beginning with the rabble that congregated in the mountain caves.

He died, of course, as dirt poor as a dog.

"One down!" he said, while struggling.

ذ

thal
9th letter
as a number, 700
in a sequence, the 25th
first letter of ذهل, to forget, and ذكر, to remember

*The best things in life
are those that don't serve
any purpose.*
(Zuhayr)

Years before, when I had been stealing books from a stall on Rua do Carmo, just as I was going to pocket a Latin version of *Almagest* by Ptolemy; I was surprised by a man's rough voice:

"Are you an astronomer, sir?"

I replied that I was not, that my interest in those things was merely literary, but I suspected that he was the astronomer.

"Actually, I teach physics classes at night school."

I deftly steered the conversation towards the problems with time-travel machines. They were limited: the traditional model of science fiction narratives, in which a machine allowed an individual to advance to the future and return to the past, frequently interfering in history, was inconceivable in strictly physical terms.

"In any theory of the universe, space and time are

interdependent factors. It is impossible for matter to travel in time without traveling in space. And vice versa."

I applied this principle to the stories told by the Lebanese man (the one with the kibbe), to conclude that they were all false. And I reached, at last, the essential conclusion: could light particles – in the same way that they fall on objects and, by reflection, bring their image to our eyes – not travel indefinitely through space?

"Without a doubt. Infinitely, if space were infinite. Until reaching the limit of space and time, in the inverse hypothesis."

I asked, also, if an image formed on Earth could be reflected in the confines of the universe and return to be observed in the same place. I wanted to know details: approximate distance from the point of reflection and the time interval between the two observations. I gave the conclusions that I could infer from *Qafiya*. He laughed.

"Only if the image travelled faster than the speed of light. In existing theories, this is still impossible."

I left the stall with two conquests: the *Almagest* by Ptolemy and the certainty that the universe permitted velocities faster than that of light (a thing that the night-school students would never dream of being possible).

I no longer doubted that the eye of Jadah was nothing more than a mirror, constructed out of any material, capable of reflecting, in a specific astronomical configuration, to the same point where they were formed, images that move much faster than light.

An objection could be raised: the prophetess detailed, from the eye of Jadah, not just al-Ghatash's movements at the Sand Oasis (which would be plausible) but also the poet's journey through the desert (which would be absurd, as she had not observed the sky in these places).

But this is just a ruse by the old woman: what she actually saw were the scenes at the oasis; the rest she knew from the verses of the *Qafiya* itself, whose echo al-Ghatash affirms to have left "everywhere".[18]

Therefore, only one problem remained: if the eye of Jadah was

---

18. Consult chapter ـﻟ, page 69.

only a type of mirror, if those who looked into it did not actually travel through time, but could just watch scenes that had occurred – at a maximum – up to half an hour ago, there could be no divergence between the lived fact and the image captured in the sky.

Therefore, the *Qafiya* contained the following errors: when al-Ghatash arrives at the village where he first encounters the crippled prophetess, he undoes a layer of his turban; in the eye of Jadah (seen by the old woman) this gesture is omitted. In the attack by the Ghurab on the Monastery of the Cave, Macários is on the same step as *Abba* Chacur and Dhu Suyuf wields one sabre; the eye of Jadah shows Mácarios a step above and Dhu Suyuf with two sabres. During the experience in the desert, the men take a dog; but numerous dogs bark against the attack by the jackals in the image recreated by the eye of Jadah.

Could it be that this reflected image returns with defects? Or is it our own perception of the facts that creates distortions? And what should we make of the incident at Najran, in which Macários testified that al-Ghatash had gone into the Ghurab's tents?[19]

---

19. Consult chapters ط, ك, and ث, on pages 69, 87 and 167 respectively.

excursion:

The oracular labyrinth

If you care to listen to one of these popular storytellers, in the marketplaces and cafes of Arab cities, you will certainly hear of a fantastical woman, who always appears dressed in black from head to toe, covered by a diaphanous veil of the same colour, and who steals, kills, incites adultery, spreads disease and disseminates every kind of evil, appearing and disappearing so suddenly that she is considered to be a female genie.

In truth, this entity goes by the name of Sayda; and she is a human being.

She must have been born in the century before al-Ghatash, to one of the pagan tribes that roamed the region of Qudayd, where there was a famous rock shrine to Manat, god of destiny, who leads one to death.

Sayda, still a girl, spent a lot of time with the god's priests. From them she heard the oracle of her own end.

Youth is incompatible with death: Sayda wanted to confirm this prophecy and appeared again in front of Manat; only this time, disguised, as if she were a man. It is not known how many times she repeated the stunt, just altering the disguise. They say that she even cut her hair, plucked out her left eye, amputated some fingers and toes.

The oracles differed in form, but they had the same meaning. Sayda, then, resolved to challenge the god. She did not just want to contradict the oracles; she intended becoming immune to death.

It is not known exactly how, but Sayda came to infiltrate herself among the pilgrims of Manat and to hear all of their destinies. Therefore she made a great discovery: in addition to confirming that an indeterminate number of oracles can possess only one interpretation (as in her case), she realised that there were a maximum number of possible interpretations, corresponding to exactly 3,732,480 personal destinies.

Sayda catalogued all of them and came to write them in the shifting sands of the desert. Notwithstanding this, Sayda's memory was like an inscription in stone; and she, conversant with the 3,732,480 destinies, could escape from not only hers, but from all of them.

According to the testimony of the sands, each one of the 3,732,480 destinies constituted a labyrinth. Death was certainly inevitable; but people with the same destinies do not necessarily arrive at them along the same path.

What made Sayda immortal was discovering the point of contact between the 3,732,480 labyrinths – which allowed her to leap from one to another, before dying. It was possible to do this, sometimes switching hands before bringing bread to her mouth, suddenly changing direction as she walked, making some or another irrelevant gesture or even stealing, killing, inciting adultery, spreading diseases, disseminating evil.

This deserves a side note. It was on the basis of the story of Sayad that erudite theoreticians analysed the number 3,732,480, established to be equivalent to the expression $3 \times 5 \times 12^5$. This is the number of possible combinations between the seven heavenly bodies employed in ancient astrology and the twelve signs of the zodiac.

These scholars are the ones truly responsible for the theory that all of humanity, from the first man to today's population, amounts to only 3,732,480 people. The rest, this immense human legion, are bodies only, endowed with false consciousness. The scholars' only problem is that they do not know how to distinguish the real people from these automated bodies, who think they are people.

But none of this is proven. What is known is that Sayda lives and that Manat is no longer worshipped in Qudayd.

To defeat death, Sayda participated in all of the destinies. It is sad, but we only remember her when she causes us harm. I don't believe we can judge her. Her error is roaming a labyrinth. Every crime is a legitimate defence.

dhad
15th letter
as a number, 800
in a sequence, the 26th
first letter of ضب, hatred and ضحكة, laughter

I am immortal:
I will never know
when I have died.
(Harith bin Hilliza)

Macários' dog, after smelling the rags of the crippled raven's clothes, barked towards the heights of the Belvedere Rock – an ancient fortified minaret built to prevent Abyssinian invasions. It was there, on those summits, in that desolate place, that the prophetess was hidden.

I whipped my camel towards where the Ghurab tribe was encamped. Her sweat carved channels in the sand like torrents sculpt riverbeds. She sweated urine, sweated milk, sweated blood, until she fell exhausted over al-Muthanni's shadow.

"The raven lives among the ruins of Belvedere Rock."

Ghurab mares followed the trail of blood, milk, urine and sweat. Macários, who arrived afterwards, had encountered them on his way.

"They are following the right path. Soon Layla will be yours."

I looked at the embroidered rugs that hid the women's tents, but I glimpsed only one thousand one hundred black horses with green eyes. In their midst, Dhu Suyuf.

"I have just added the last stallion to the herd. This is the bride price that I promised for Layla when a Labwa dog carries Sabah away."

Only then did I understand why the sheik had waited so long. For the first time, I admired an enemy. I gave thanks for the agreement that gave me the opportunity to steal two brides from a man who fought with both hands.

Suddenly, a dust cloud arose on the horizon, announcing the rumble, coming from the direction of Belvedere Rock. At the same time, something similar to a human figure seemed to take shape in the opposite distance, in the depths of the desert of ruddy sands. The images drew near like drops running down from two points in a funnel.

It was not long before I recognised the Ghurab horsemen. But I refused to believe what my eyes saw in the other direction.

"This is what we found at Belvedere Rock!"

And they threw raven's bodies at my face – all that Macários' dog could sniff in the piece of the crippled prophetess's cloak, who now appeared quite distinctly, limping with her crooked walk and, before the incredulous gaze of the living, entered a Ghurab tent on her own two legs.

parameter:

Labid

Al-Ghatash died young. Labid belongs to the small group of the *muammarun* – poets who lived until they reached one hundred years of age. Labid could have reached one hundred and fifty or one thousand five hundred – it is a question of zeros, which in Arabic script are represented by a small dot.

Labid lived for so long that he eventually became a contemporary of the Prophet and converted to Islam.

The name "Labid" has the same root as "Lubad" – the seventh vulture associated with the seven lives of the legendary scholar Luqman. The Bedouin believe that the vulture is an animal of extraordinary longevity. Each of Luqman's seven lives lasts as long as the life of one of his vultures, successively, which guaranteed him a longevity of more than seven centuries. No one took seriously the hypothesis that Labid was a vulture.

But before being an elder sculpted by the finite wisdom of the world, Labid was a boy, was a man, fought in the wars of Ignorance and was a hero, as the Arab poets should be.

There is a curious episode in Labid's biography. During the eternal conflict that involved the tribe of Ghassan, allied with the Byzantines, and the tribe of Lakhm, who supported the Persians, Labid, possessor of immense prestige among the Lakhm, sent the tribe's sheik a generous present, as proof of vassalage and alliance. It was one thousand chests of stones and metal, presented on one thousand beautiful, richly decorated horses, which also formed part of the present.

When the Lakhm sheik received them, one thousand horsemen hidden in the chests attacked, armed. Among the pillaged goods was the sheik's head.

Who does not see in this episode the historic origin of Homer's myth of the Trojan horse? This is the greatest evidence of Labid's antiquity.

Labid was a wise man, a poet, a horseman, he fought, he drank, he loved, he played, he betrayed. His Suspended Poem – one of the most beautiful, certainly – composed in a thoroughly complex rhyme that repeats itself in no less than eighty-eight verses, is the condensed form of all the motives, implicit and explicit, of pre-Islamic poetry. I was able to translate only the worst excerpts.

Traces of the tents fade away, the vastness of the deserts empties; even the caves, where the hyenas live;
the riverbeds, that flow from the mountain, are bare, faded, like ancient inscriptions on stone.
The torrents exposed the ruins, like one restoring an ancient inscription.
So I stopped and interrogated those rocks. But how to interrogate deaf immortals, whose language is incomprehensible?

The rest of the poem evokes the traditional scene of the parting of the women, who leave like wild cows, like white gazelles, until the mirage dissolves and they are just marks in the sand.

Abruptly, Labid switches from the theme of amorous separation to describing the camel. There is an immortal verse:

The best lover is the one who most easily breaks the reins of love.

From these erotic experiences that endured for centuries, Labid came to form a valid thesis on the female personality. His Suspended Poem is about the camel, the wild female donkey, the female oryx, and the mare. Each one of them is a metaphor for a type of woman.

Apart from this, there is a scene in a tavern, a tribute to the tribe, war and the hunt.

Muhammed was dead when Labid proclaimed *There is no god but God* and renounced poetry. Many Bedouins came to Labid to ask him why.

"There is only one God. There is only one Book. Blessings upon the Prophet whose sole miracle is the Book," was his answer.

I would have said that there is only one Poem, Labid's poem, reproduced by the Arabs on the Black Stone.

Labid's conversion symbolises the end of pre-Islamic poetry. The Age of Ignorance had ended. And I believe that Labid, wrinkled by time, immense yet finite, was none other than the very vulture Lubad. The difference is just in the vowels. Only that, unlike zero, in the ancient Arabic orthography the vowels were not written.

ظ

thoh
17th letter
as a number, 900
in a sequence, the 27th
first letter of ظل, shadow, and ظن, faith

I do not love everything that I have,
but I do have everything that I love.
(Nabigha)

By specific reference to Belvedere Rock it could be deduced that the oasis where al-Muthanni's people must have been was Bab al-Rimal, the Door of Sands, which was situated at the limits of the vast and impassable Rub al-Khali, or the Desolate Quadrant, the most terrible of Arab deserts, a grave of red sand for those Bedouins who ventured into it.

This is the scene where the final movements of *Qafiya al-Qaf* unfold: the death of al-Ghatash and the extinction of the Ghurab race – everything that the crippled prophetess had predicted; or, who knows, prompted.

This passage of the poem explicitly shows that the character of the prophetess, constructed in the image of ravens and crows, belonged to the Ghurab lineage, but was exiled from the tribal circle and put on them the curse of an exile that would bring everyone to their end. According to the old woman's own words, this would happen when she returned to the tents on her own feet.

The sheik of the Ghurab believed he could avoid the bad omen if he captured her by his own hand and dragged her back, tied to the saddle of a mare. But destiny has ideas of its own.

At the instant when al-Muthanni pierced the prophetess' body with all the arrows in his quiver and al-Ghatash realised that he had lost the means of fulfilling the third condition, another throng dotted the horizon. The Ghurab raised the standards, unsheathed the sabres and arranged the horses in a line of combat. But they were rapidly surrounded by the horsemen of Salih and federated tribes, as numerous as the grains in a fistful of sand.

Many died; others fled. The only way out was the Desolate Quadrant. They were not a tribe who ran away. They were terrified men who fled in disarray: the predicted disappearance of the sons of Ghurab.

Al-Ghatash, then, accompanied by Macários (it was on this journey that the monk memorised the final verses of the *Qafiya*), headed off in pursuit of Layla, who had not hesitated in opting to ride pillion on Dhu Suyuf's mare.

The poet entered the desert. An improbable eleven days were spent on the trail of that veiled woman. Macários warned that this is the day on which the eye of Jadah would shine in the sky again. Night drew near with the forewarning of a tempest.

From behind a small dune, Layla and Dhu Suyuf emerge, whose arrows cause the son of Labwa's camel to fall. A gust of wind arises. Layla's veils do not come loose. She disappears in a cavalcade.

Macários cries out for al-Ghatash, who insists on continuing on foot and on solving, once and for all, the riddle of Qaf, contemplating the eye of Jadah.

The monk decides to return alone, first indicating the exact position where the phenomenon will occur. He had barely turned his back, when he heard the poet lauding the beauty of a mare of the Ghurab, black mane, thick lips, wide hips.

Exactly like the day on which he had glimpsed the face of Sabah, the woman he had been searching for and who was already his.

excursion:

Amir's dancers

Love, in the form we know of today, is a Hindu concept, if not Chinese. But it did not arise out of these peoples' sensory experiences, as they have come to affirm. In its slow evolution, love was considerably influenced by pure eroticism, essentially physical. In this field, it is necessary to recognise the Arab precedent.

During the times when the extinct Fadua tribe dominated the sandy expanses and most of the oases that stretched from the peninsula's north to its south, Bedouin clans were still commanded by women. As occurs between animal species, power was exercised by the more beautiful sex.

It fell to the women to attract men, if they desired them, who were forbidden from taking the initiative. Frequently, disputes over the men generated conflict, not infrequently degenerating into tribal wars – such was the importance of men in matrilineal descent.

Although the moveable goods and herds were also considered, the command normally rested with the woman who had the greatest number of husbands. To a degree, it was the number of husbands that defined a Bedouin woman's degree of wealth.

Kidnappings of men were very common. Mutilations as well, of the husbands of others. But Arab women soon realised that they could exert a more enduring power over the desired object, through sexual attraction. As this tendency took root, the most elaborate erotic art in Antiquity, of which we are aware, arose.

The advances made since then in medicine, hygiene, erotology are incalculable. Arabs were the first to identify and sensually explore the clitoris. From their experiences with animals, they also discovered the technique of artificial insemination – which would result in spectacular genetic improvement of equine breeds, to the point of turning the Arab horse into the most perfect example of its species.

It is not necessary to mention the development of the crafts of perfumes, dyes, and jewellery. The textile arts experienced identical expansion, principally in the creation of veils – which at the time only served to protect the face and hair from the rigours of the sun and from sandstorms.

In tents pervaded with incense, perfumed and painted Bedouins, dressed in beautiful clothing, adorned with the richest of ornaments, subjected the men to ever more sophisticated pleasures, anxious to succeed over their opponents.

In public duels, conducted in the middle of the encampments, the women danced to seduce and entrance young men available for marriage.

It was specifically during this time that Arabic music developed a new genre – the *raqs*, known in the West as the "belly dance" – based on a very lively percussion and a solo *rababah* fiddle. There was no singing: the subjective expression was exclusively choreographic.

Legend credits a certain Amir with the invention of the *raqs*, both the rhythm as well as the dance. With unusual speed, the novelty spread through the desert and came to be the only genre employed in female performances, in front of eligible young men.

Amir perfected the elements of his creation: he conceived delicate swaying of the head, of the neck, of the thorax; he considerably expanded the repertoire of gestures; gave sophistication to the variety of steps; and – principally – lent unusual dimension to a vast gamut of movements of the hip and belly.

Arab princesses demanded more and Amir came to conceive of

a language. Rather, a script. Inspired by the Hebrew alphabet, which he came to know during his trips through Egypt, he created a system according to which each choreographed movement came to correspond to a syllable from the Arabic language: from there, the succession of movements formed words and sentences. He secretly revealed this invention to each dancer.

Bedouin women used these volatile letters, that unwritten script, to promise pleasure and elation, protection and wealth, in sentences ever more intricate, in a never-ending competition. Only that the men, foolishly, did not notice anything new and remained as prisoners to the ancient aesthetic.

It was then that the phenomenon occurred: the dancers, coming from all the corners of Arabia, began to look only for Amir, only wanting Amir, to perform only for Amir.

That humble man, a slave according to some, who could have been handsome, came to be – for having created that cypher – the only man capable of understanding a new concept of beauty.

It is easy to understand why Arab tribes, from that point on, came to be dominated by the men, rebelling against the females who had seduced them and then opted for Amir.

One day, as could have been foreseen, Amir was castrated, tortured and killed by hostile, brutal Bedouins, who then began the hunt for women and never imagined that they could be so powerful.

غ

ghayn
19th letter
as a number, 1,000
in a sequence, the 28th
beginning of غسق, twilight, and غرق, shipwreck

The best blind man is he
who wants to see.
(Anonymous)

Well, this is the final step. The eye of Jadah cast back to al-Ghatash the image of the scene that the poet had just lived, with a slight distortion: Dhu Suyuf and Layla arising from behind the dunes, the death of the camel, the wind blowing, Layla's veil – this time – lifting, and the face of Sabah, which looks at the poet for the last time before disappearing in the cavalcade.

Macários abandoned al-Ghatash. He had in his memory all of *Qafiya al-Qaf*, whose final verses he had just heard.

But not even these final verses, becoming more beautiful with each reading, succeeded in impressing the 'inauthenticists'. On the contrary, they believe that – exactly because of this ending – *Qafiya* is shown to be nothing more than a huge joke, painstakingly created with fine erudition by a contemporary forger.

Their principal argument rests on an analysis of the characters' names: *Sabah* means "morning" – a metaphor for someone who receives light on an uncovered face; and Layla, "night" – which is associated with the darkness of a face always hidden.

This would attest to the fact, for some, that both are the same person, whose name varies according to whether or not they have the veil. In addition, when the eye of Jadah shows Layla unveiled, it is Sabah's face that al-Ghatash gazes upon.

What reinforces this thesis is the fact that the *Qafiya*, after the rejection of Sabah, simply does not mention her and never again refers to an encounter between two sisters, even when the Ghurab and the Labwa were together in Mecca, during the month of pilgrimage.

I believe that the lapse is due to the probable sale of Sabah as a slave after her rejection. I read somewhere about an Arab dancer named Sabah, who provoked jealousy and death among Roman soldiers of the Jaffa garrison. But this is just a hypothesis.

It is contrary to another, much more damaging, interpretation, because it brings ridicule on *Qafiya*, which always disgusts me. According to this theme, sheik al-Muthanni (which can be translated as *that which duplicates, that which doubles*) received this name for having been the father of twins; and the poet al-Ghatash (from a root which means *to be dark, to have a weak vision, to not observe*), being almost incapable of distinguishing two different faces, was called this for the huge mistake of having seen Layla and thinking it was Sabah.

I cannot accept this debasement of poetry. I cannot imagine such a perverse joke. I cannot believe that my grandfather Naguib, when he would look seriously through the telescope, when he affirmed that it was possible to move back in time, had not carried out the experiment, had not already confirmed the manifestation of the eye of Jadah.

It was because of this that I studied the science of the stars in depth, that I learned to work with mariner's quadrants, sextants, astrolabes, telescopes, almanacs, celestial maps. But still I did not have the courage to undertake the experience.

I am afraid of seeing a different version of the *Qafiya*. I am afraid of seeing a different version of myself.

Postscript

Those knowledgeable about Arab literature will have noticed that my translations of pre-Islamic poetry are not exactly literal.

I tried, of course, to be more faithful to the image than to the content.

Some will also say that certain passages of these poets' lives cannot be found in any of the known compilations.

I hope that these critics truly understand the nature of myths.

And do not accuse me of having been false: being false is the essence of things.

The stories of this book are for João.